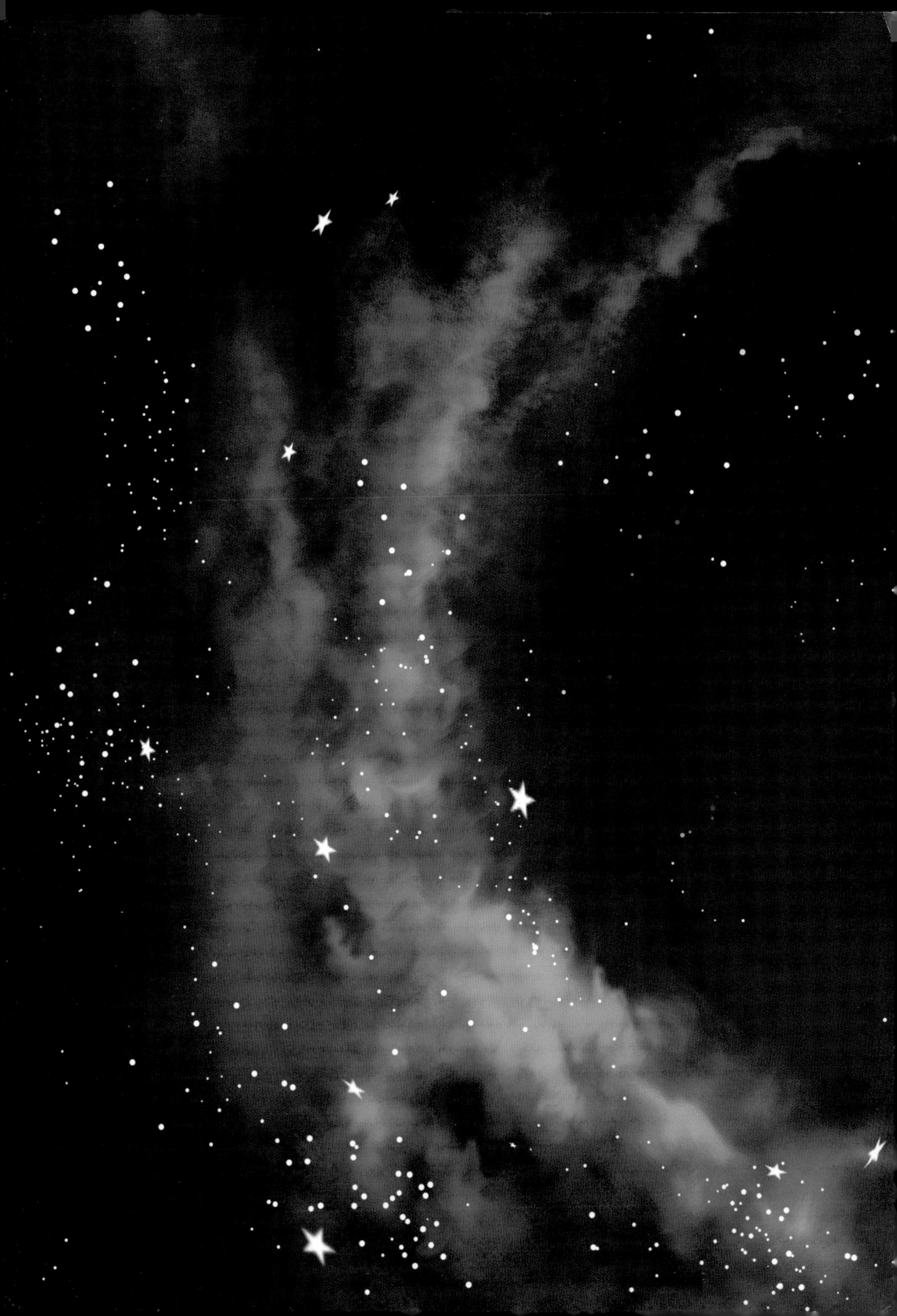

My dear Rose,

Here I am with Fox, traveling through the stars on the trail
of the Snake. We just left Zephyr and Foehn on the planet
of the Eolians. Thanks to them, I've learned that we must
always encourage the ones we love to follow not our dreams
but their own.

I'm sorry, but I'll have to leave you now. Another star system
is on the point of being destroyed. The Snake has wasted
no time! Now it seems he's on the planet of the Firebird…
Fox is going to like that!

This journey is long, and we're so far away from you…
I think about you every day when I watch the sunset. And
you, my Rose, what are you dreaming of?

The Little Prince

First American edition published in 2012 by Graphic Universe™.

Le Petit Prince ™

based on the masterpiece by Antoine de Saint-Exupéry

© 2012 LPPM
An animated series based on the novel *Le Petit Prince* by Antoine de Saint-Exupéry
Developed for television by Matthieu Delaporte, Alexandre de la Patellière, and Bertrand Gatignol
Directed by Pierre-Alain Chartier

© 2012 ÉDITIONS GLÉNAT
Copyright © 2012 by Lerner Publishing Group, Inc., for the current edition

Graphic Universe™
A division of Lerner Publishing Group, Inc.
241 First Avenue North
Minneapolis, MN 55401 U.S.A.

Website address: www.lernerbooks.com

Library of Congress Cataloging-in-Publication Data

Dorison, Guillaume.
 [Planète de L'Oiseau de Feu. English]
 The planet of the Firebird / by Julien Magnat ; adapted by Guillaume Dorison ; based on the masterpiece by Antoine de Saint-Exupéry ; illustrated by Élyum Studio, Diane Fayolle, and Jérôme Benoit ; translation, Carol Klio Burrell. — 1st American ed.
  p. cm. — (The little prince ; #02)
  ISBN: 978—0—7613—8752—7 (lib. bdg. : alk. paper)
  1. Graphic novels. I. Fayolle, Diane. II. Benoit, Jérôme. III. Saint-Exupéry, Antoine de, 1900—1944. Petit Prince. IV. Élyum Studio. V. Petit Prince (Television program) VI. Title.
 PZ7.7.D67Pk 2012
 741.5'944—dc23   2011047659

Manufactured in the United States of America
1 — DP — 7/15/12

THE NEW ADVENTURES
BASED ON THE MASTERPIECE BY ANTOINE DE SAINT-EXUPÉRY

The Little Prince

THE PLANET OF THE FIREBIRD

Based on the animated series and an original story by Julien Magnat

Design: Élyum Studio
Adaptation: Guillaume Dorison
Artistic Direction: Didier Poli
Art: Diane Fayolle
Backgrounds: Jérôme Benoit
Coloring: Digikore
Editing: Didier Poli
Editorial Consultant: Didier Convard

Translation: Carol Burrell

Graphic Universe™ • Minneapolis • New York

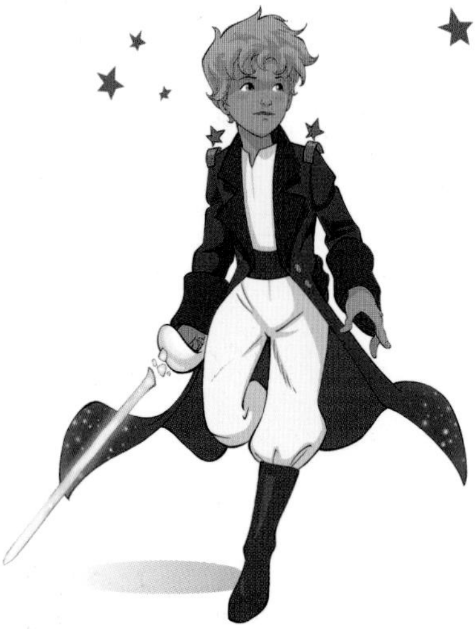

THE LITTLE PRINCE

The Little Prince has extraordinary gifts. His sense of wonder allows him to discover what no one else can see. The Little Prince can communicate with all the beings in the universe, even the animals and plants. His powers grow over the course of his adventures.

The Prince's uniform:
When he wears the uniform of a prince, he is more agile and quick. When faced with difficult situations, the Little Prince also carries a sword that lets him sketch and bring to life anything from his imagination.

His sketchbook:
When he is not in his Prince's clothing, the Little Prince carries a sketchbook. When he blows on the pages, they take wing and form objects that he'll find very useful.

FOX

A grouch, a trickster, and, so he says, interested only in his next meal, Fox is in reality the Little Prince's best friend. As such, he is always there to give him help, but also just as much to help him to grow and to learn about the world.

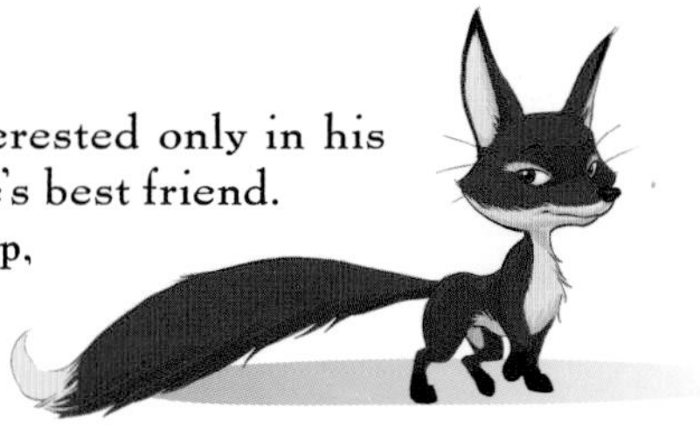

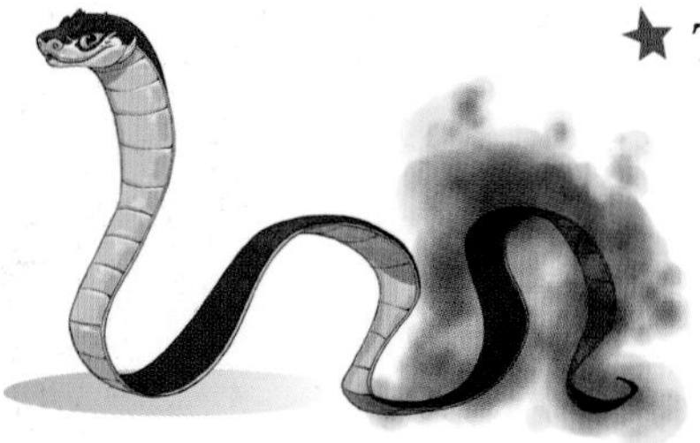

THE SNAKE

Even though the Little Prince still does not know exactly why, there can be no doubt that the Snake has set his mind to plunging the entire universe into darkness! And to accomplish his goal, this malicious being is ready to use any form of deception. However, the Snake never takes action himself. He prefers to bring out the wickedness in those beings he has chosen to bite, tempting them to put their own worlds in danger.

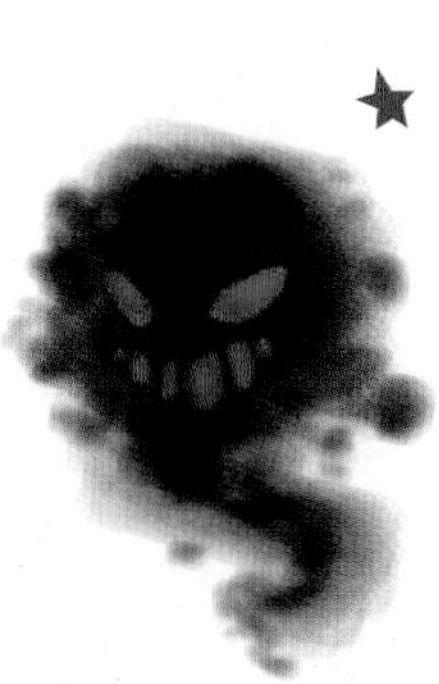

THE GLOOMIES

When people who have been "bitten" by the Snake have completely destroyed their own planets, they become Gloomies, slaves to their Snake master. The Gloomies act as a group and carry out the Serpent's most vile orders so as to get the better of the Little Prince!

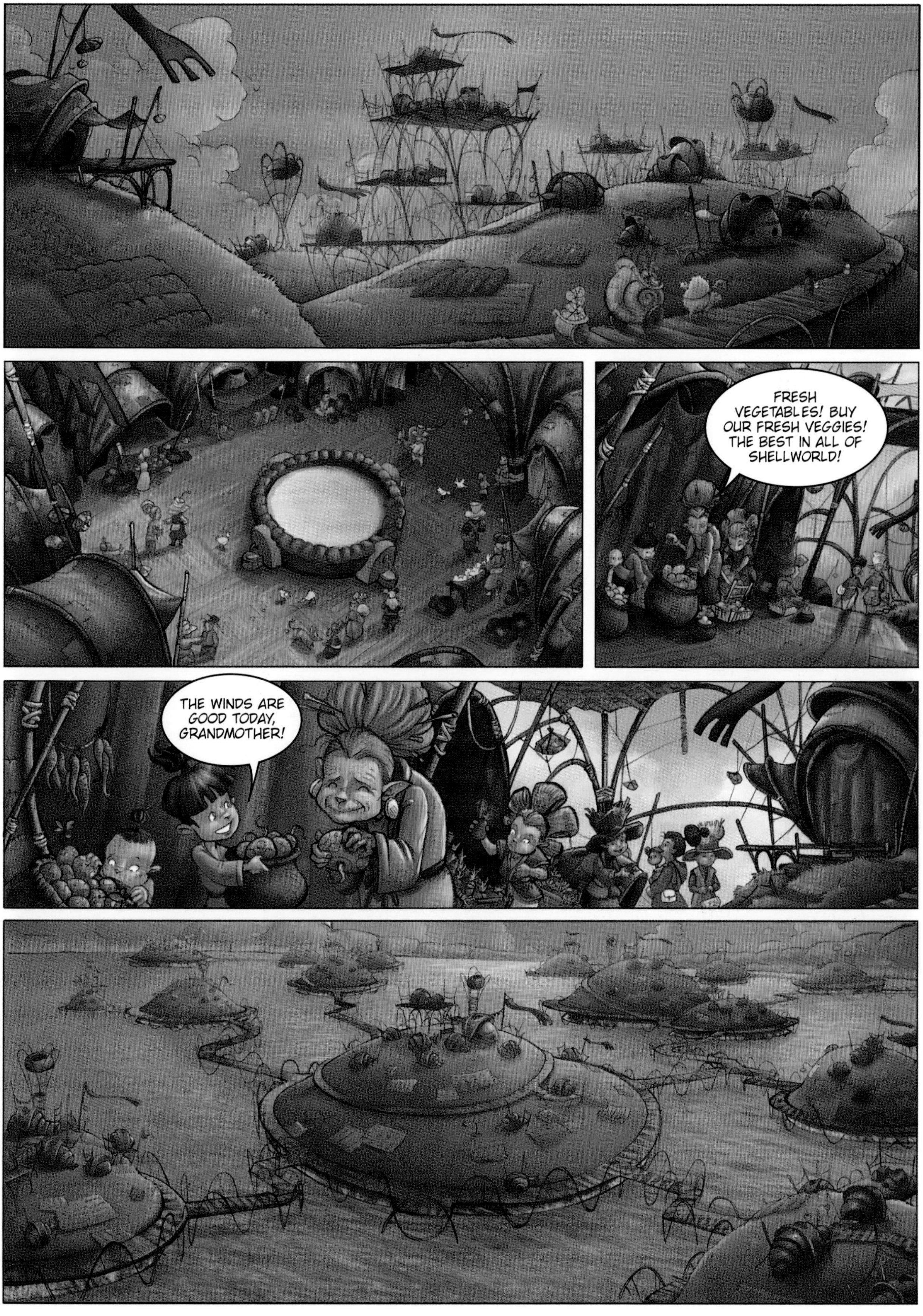
FRESH VEGETABLES! BUY OUR FRESH VEGGIES! THE BEST IN ALL OF SHELLWORLD!
THE WINDS ARE GOOD TODAY, GRANDMOTHER!

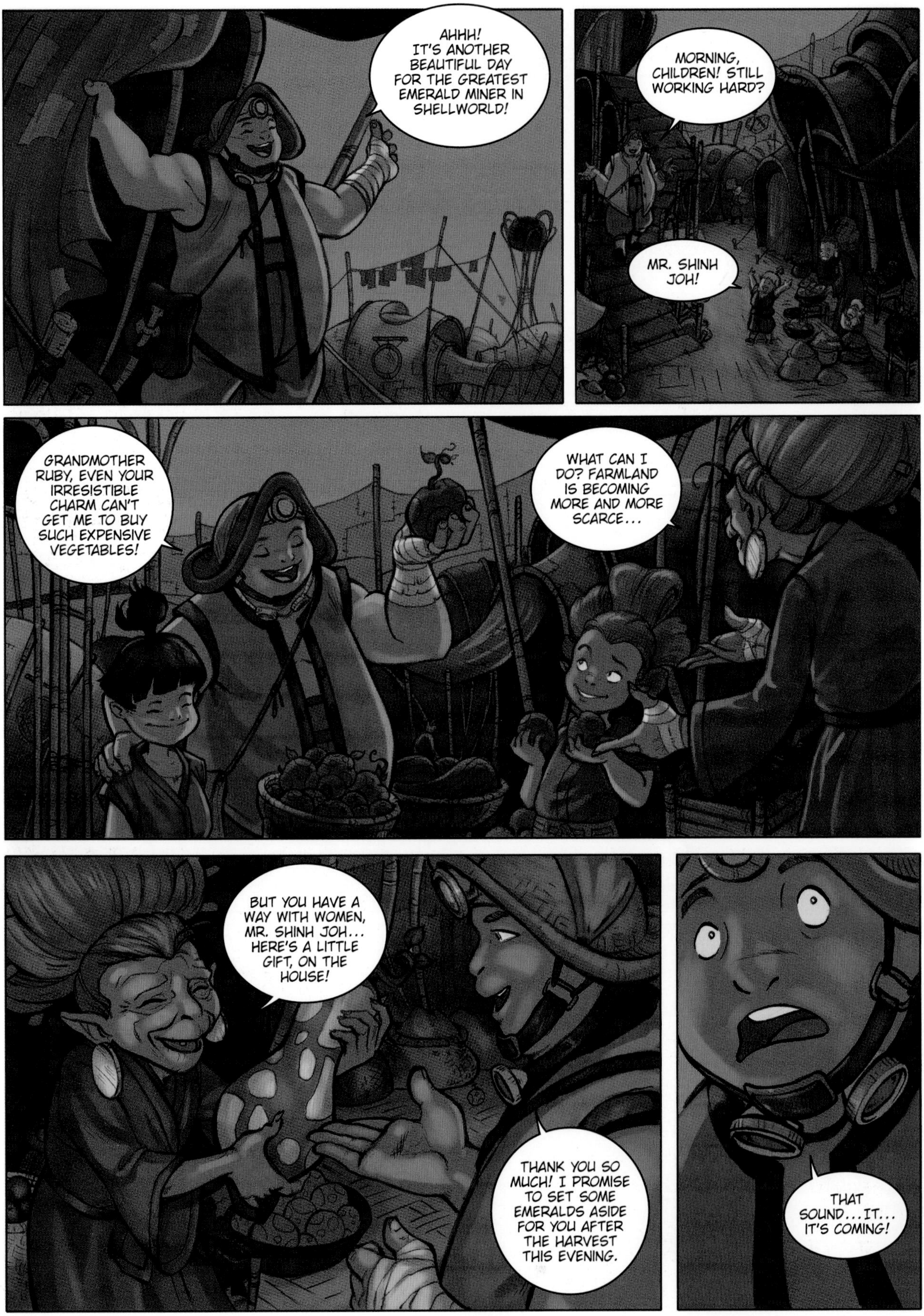
AHHH! IT'S ANOTHER BEAUTIFUL DAY FOR THE GREATEST EMERALD MINER IN SHELLWORLD!
MORNING, CHILDREN! STILL WORKING HARD?
MR. SHINH JOH!
GRANDMOTHER RUBY, EVEN YOUR IRRESISTIBLE CHARM CAN'T GET ME TO BUY SUCH EXPENSIVE VEGETABLES!
WHAT CAN I DO? FARMLAND IS BECOMING MORE AND MORE SCARCE...
BUT YOU HAVE A WAY WITH WOMEN, MR. SHINH JOH... HERE'S A LITTLE GIFT, ON THE HOUSE!
THANK YOU SO MUCH! I PROMISE TO SET SOME EMERALDS ASIDE FOR YOU AFTER THE HARVEST THIS EVENING.
THAT SOUND... IT... IT'S COMING!

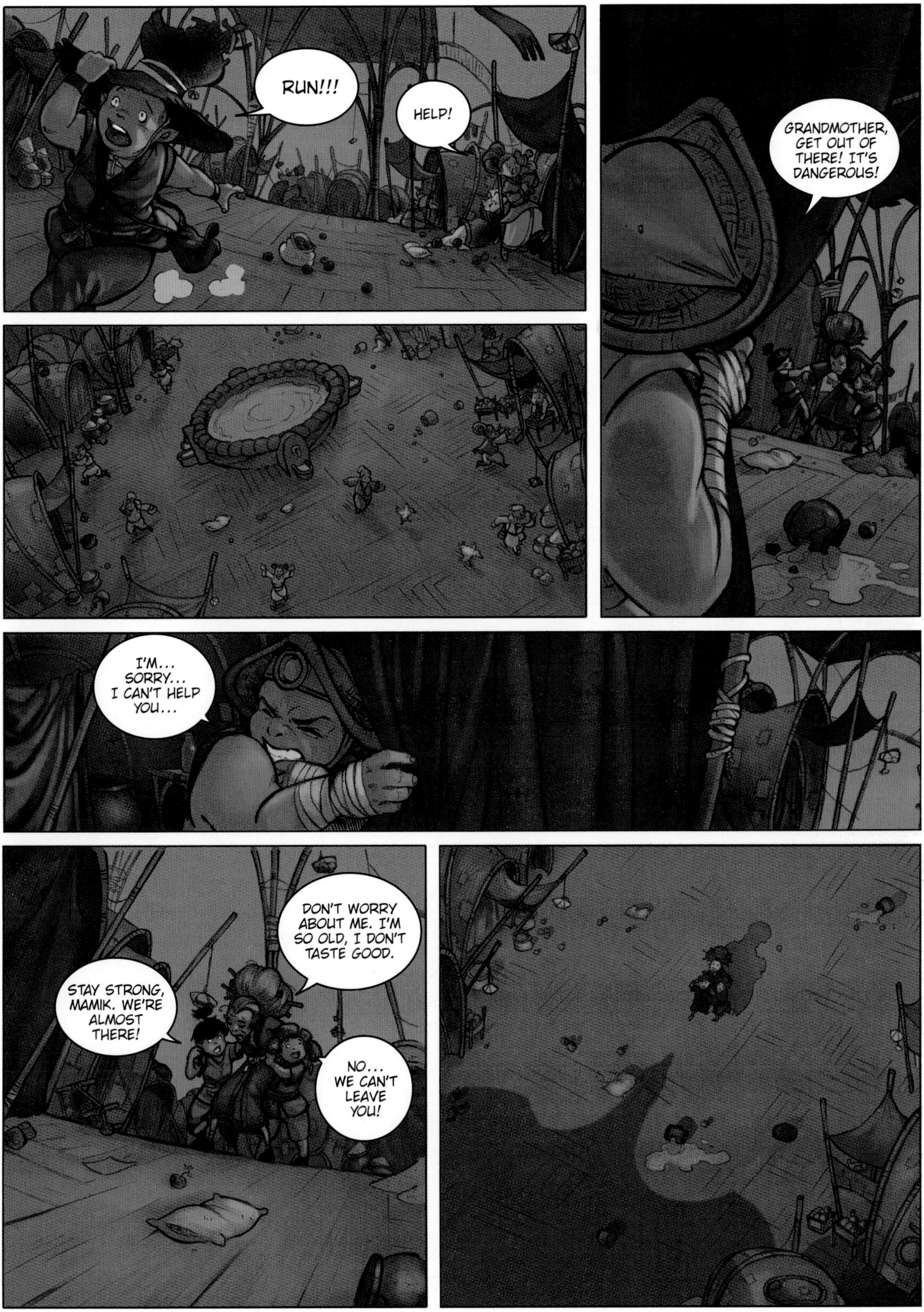
RUN!!!
HELP!
GRANDMOTHER, GET OUT OF THERE! IT'S DANGEROUS!
I'M... SORRY... I CAN'T HELP YOU...
STAY STRONG, MAMIK. WE'RE ALMOST THERE!
DON'T WORRY ABOUT ME. I'M SO OLD, I DON'T TASTE GOOD.
NO... WE CAN'T LEAVE YOU!

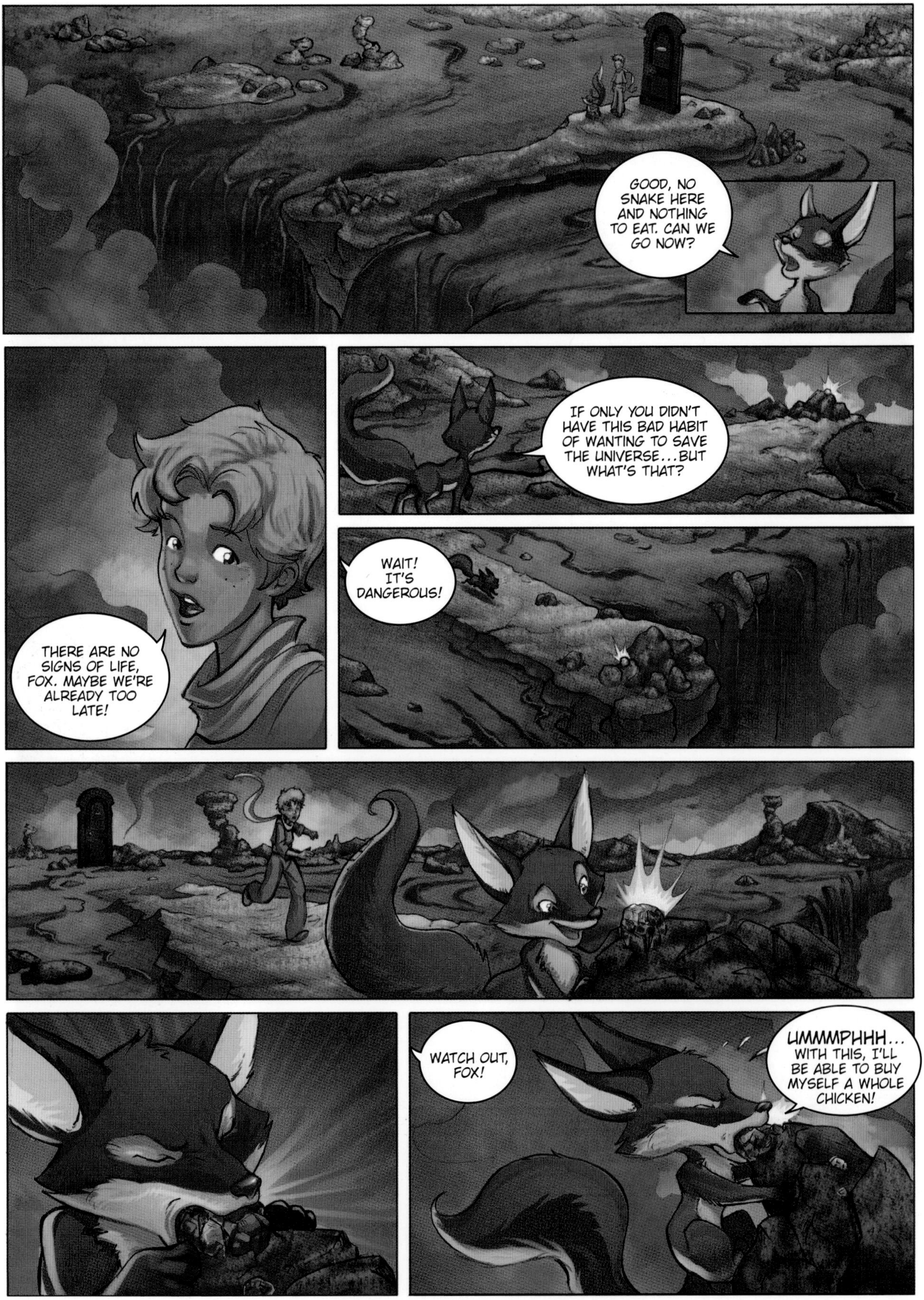
GOOD, NO SNAKE HERE AND NOTHING TO EAT. CAN WE GO NOW?
THERE ARE NO SIGNS OF LIFE, FOX. MAYBE WE'RE ALREADY TOO LATE!
IF ONLY YOU DIDN'T HAVE THIS BAD HABIT OF WANTING TO SAVE THE UNIVERSE…BUT WHAT'S THAT?
WAIT! IT'S DANGEROUS!
WATCH OUT, FOX!
UMMMPHHH… WITH THIS, I'LL BE ABLE TO BUY MYSELF A WHOLE CHICKEN!

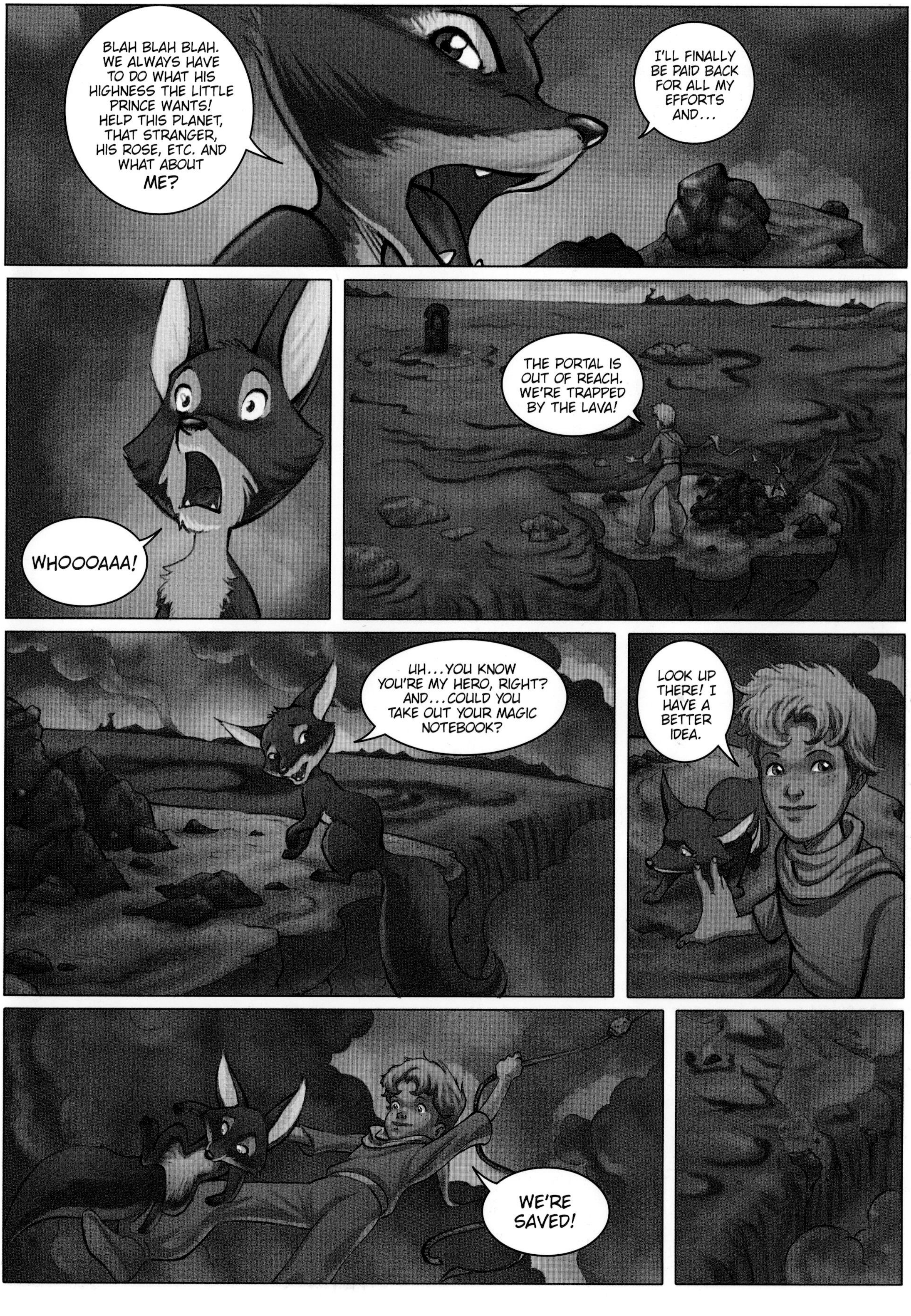
BLAH BLAH BLAH. WE ALWAYS HAVE TO DO WHAT HIS HIGHNESS THE LITTLE PRINCE WANTS! HELP THIS PLANET, THAT STRANGER, HIS ROSE, ETC. AND WHAT ABOUT ME?
I'LL FINALLY BE PAID BACK FOR ALL MY EFFORTS AND...
WHOOOAAA!
THE PORTAL IS OUT OF REACH. WE'RE TRAPPED BY THE LAVA!
UH...YOU KNOW YOU'RE MY HERO, RIGHT? AND...COULD YOU TAKE OUT YOUR MAGIC NOTEBOOK?
LOOK UP THERE! I HAVE A BETTER IDEA.
WE'RE SAVED!

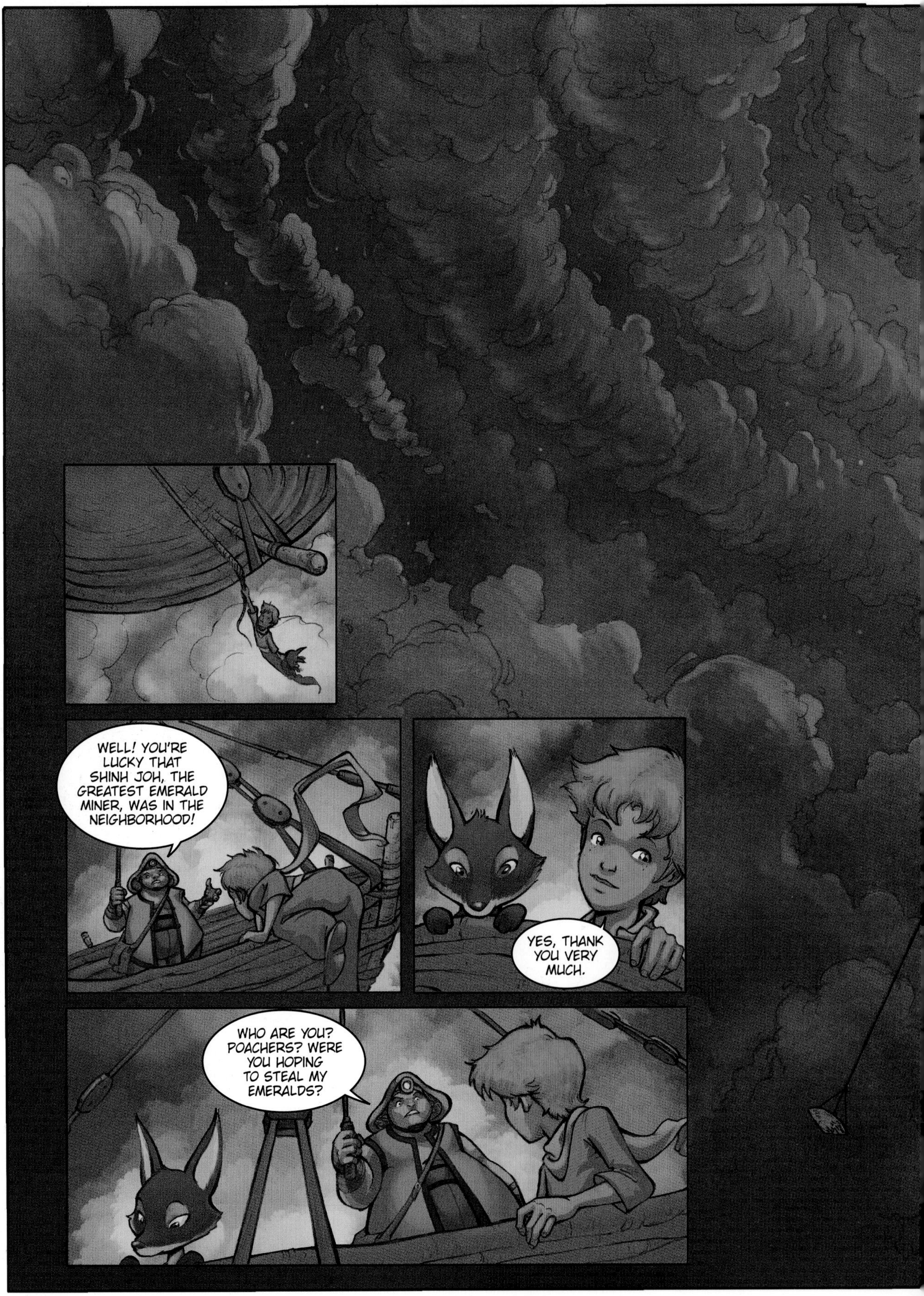
WELL! YOU'RE LUCKY THAT SHINH JOH, THE GREATEST EMERALD MINER, WAS IN THE NEIGHBORHOOD!
YES, THANK YOU VERY MUCH.
WHO ARE YOU? POACHERS? WERE YOU HOPING TO STEAL MY EMERALDS?

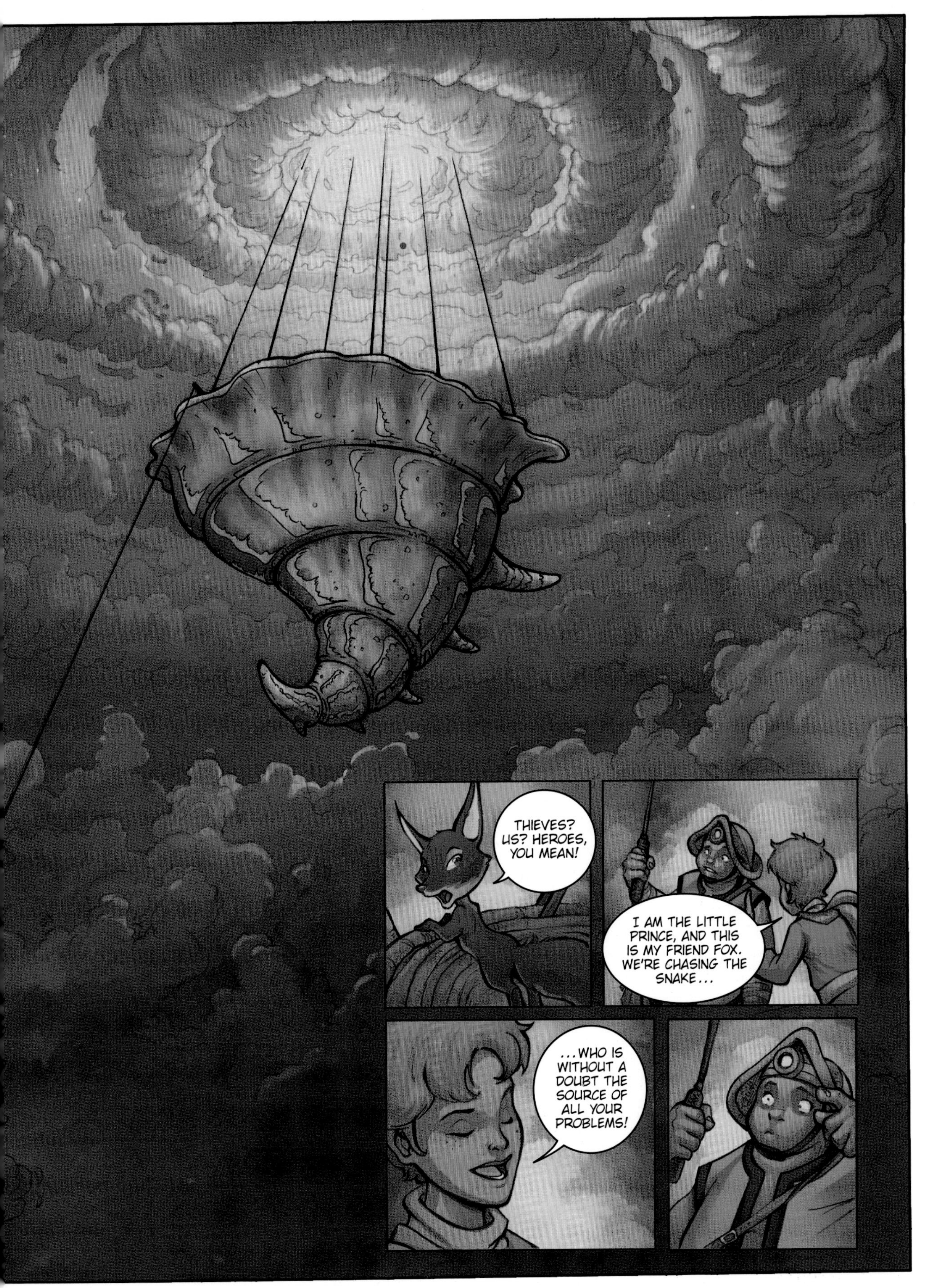
THIEVES? US? HEROES, YOU MEAN!
I AM THE LITTLE PRINCE, AND THIS IS MY FRIEND FOX. WE'RE CHASING THE SNAKE...
...WHO IS WITHOUT A DOUBT THE SOURCE OF ALL YOUR PROBLEMS!

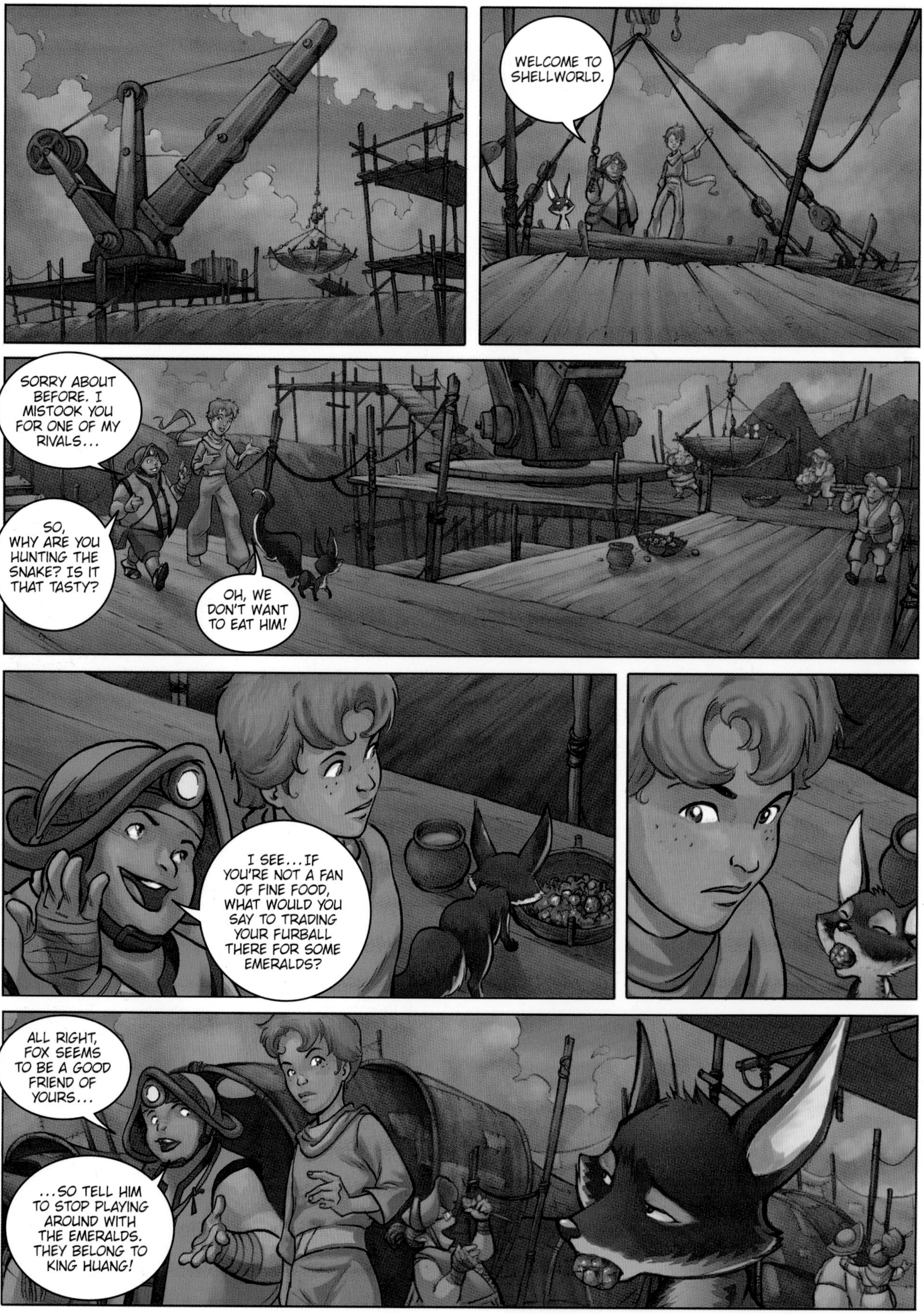

WELCOME TO SHELLWORLD.
SORRY ABOUT BEFORE. I MISTOOK YOU FOR ONE OF MY RIVALS...
SO, WHY ARE YOU HUNTING THE SNAKE? IS IT THAT TASTY?
OH, WE DON'T WANT TO EAT HIM!
I SEE... IF YOU'RE NOT A FAN OF FINE FOOD, WHAT WOULD YOU SAY TO TRADING YOUR FURBALL THERE FOR SOME EMERALDS?
ALL RIGHT, FOX SEEMS TO BE A GOOD FRIEND OF YOURS...
...SO TELL HIM TO STOP PLAYING AROUND WITH THE EMERALDS. THEY BELONG TO KING HUANG!

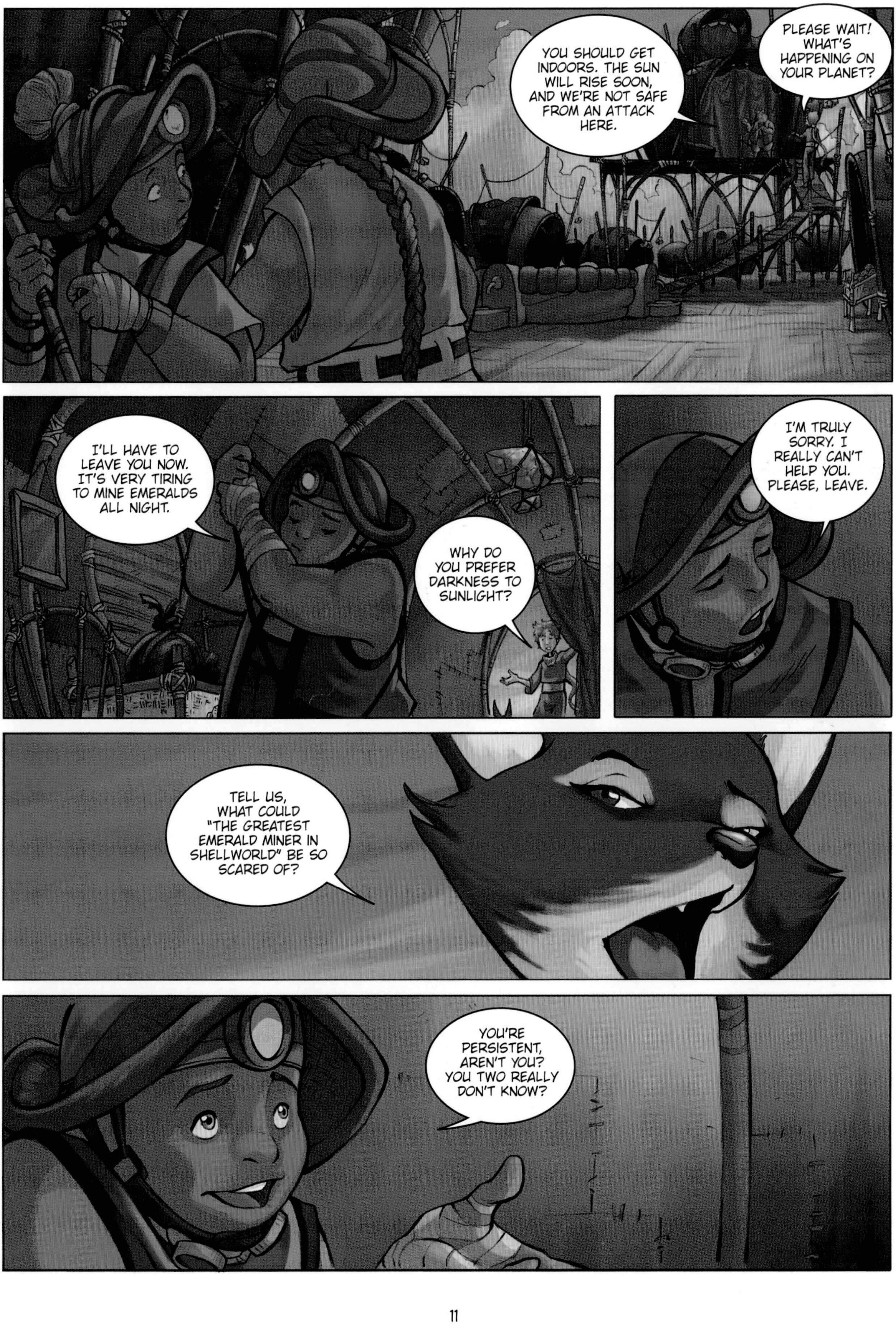
YOU SHOULD GET INDOORS. THE SUN WILL RISE SOON, AND WE'RE NOT SAFE FROM AN ATTACK HERE.
PLEASE WAIT! WHAT'S HAPPENING ON YOUR PLANET?
I'LL HAVE TO LEAVE YOU NOW. IT'S VERY TIRING TO MINE EMERALDS ALL NIGHT.
WHY DO YOU PREFER DARKNESS TO SUNLIGHT?
I'M TRULY SORRY. I REALLY CAN'T HELP YOU. PLEASE, LEAVE.
TELL US, WHAT COULD "THE GREATEST EMERALD MINER IN SHELLWORLD" BE SO SCARED OF?
YOU'RE PERSISTENT, AREN'T YOU? YOU TWO REALLY DON'T KNOW?

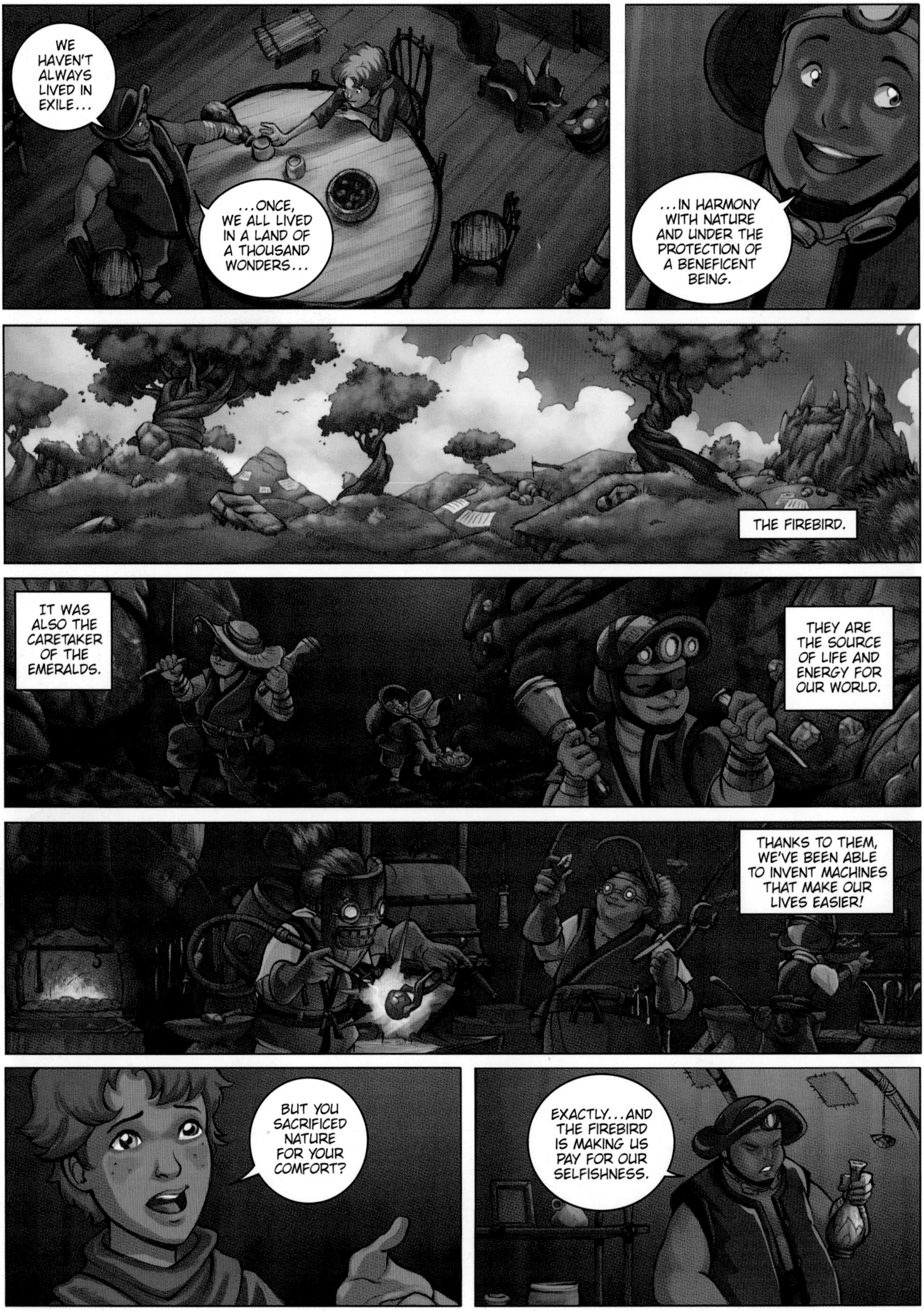
WE HAVEN'T ALWAYS LIVED IN EXILE...
...ONCE, WE ALL LIVED IN A LAND OF A THOUSAND WONDERS...
...IN HARMONY WITH NATURE AND UNDER THE PROTECTION OF A BENEFICENT BEING.
THE FIREBIRD.
IT WAS ALSO THE CARETAKER OF THE EMERALDS.
THEY ARE THE SOURCE OF LIFE AND ENERGY FOR OUR WORLD.
THANKS TO THEM, WE'VE BEEN ABLE TO INVENT MACHINES THAT MAKE OUR LIVES EASIER!
BUT YOU SACRIFICED NATURE FOR YOUR COMFORT?
EXACTLY...AND THE FIREBIRD IS MAKING US PAY FOR OUR SELFISHNESS.

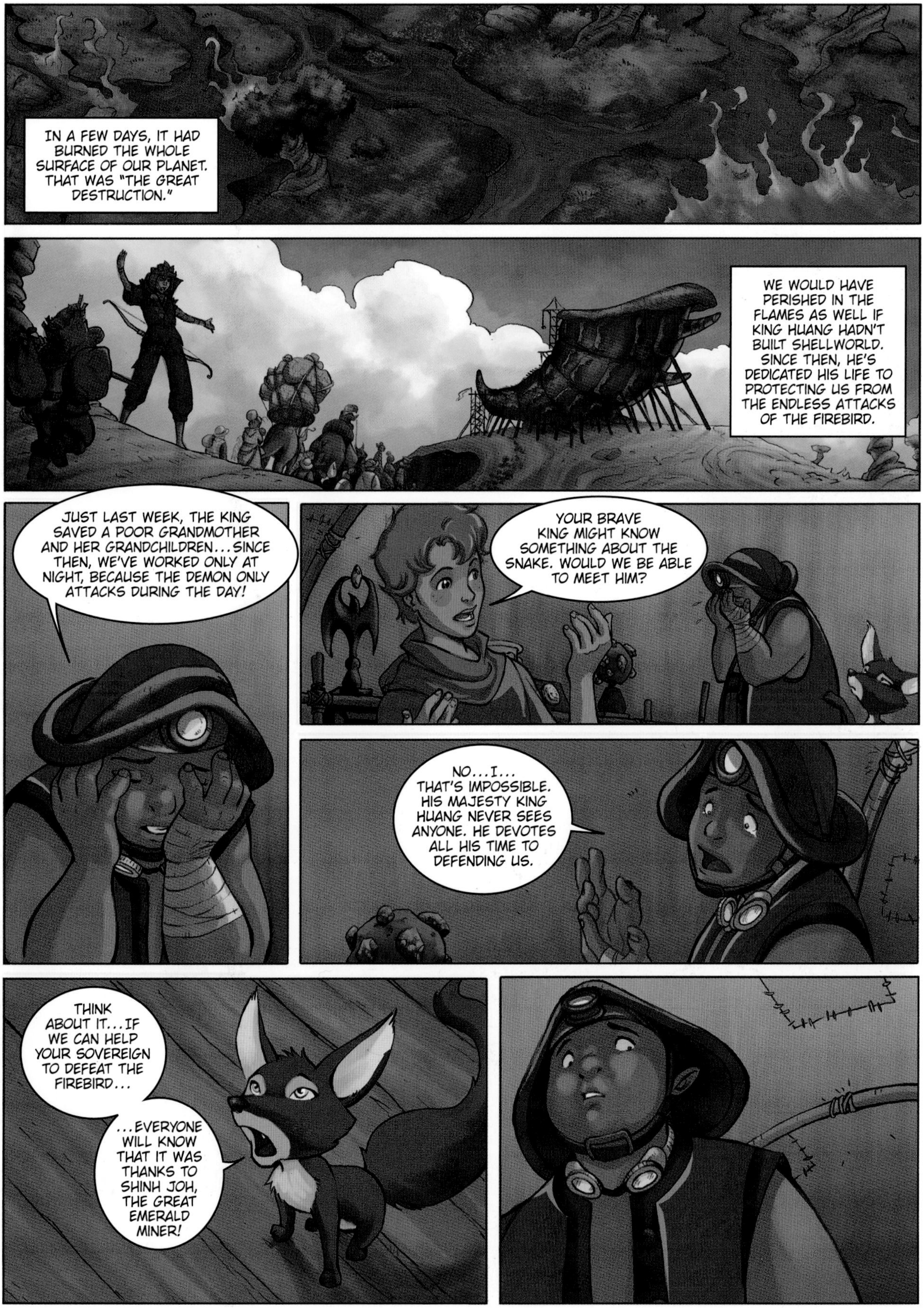
IN A FEW DAYS, IT HAD BURNED THE WHOLE SURFACE OF OUR PLANET. THAT WAS "THE GREAT DESTRUCTION."
WE WOULD HAVE PERISHED IN THE FLAMES AS WELL IF KING HUANG HADN'T BUILT SHELLWORLD. SINCE THEN, HE'S DEDICATED HIS LIFE TO PROTECTING US FROM THE ENDLESS ATTACKS OF THE FIREBIRD.
JUST LAST WEEK, THE KING SAVED A POOR GRANDMOTHER AND HER GRANDCHILDREN... SINCE THEN, WE'VE WORKED ONLY AT NIGHT, BECAUSE THE DEMON ONLY ATTACKS DURING THE DAY!
YOUR BRAVE KING MIGHT KNOW SOMETHING ABOUT THE SNAKE. WOULD WE BE ABLE TO MEET HIM?
NO... I... THAT'S IMPOSSIBLE. HIS MAJESTY KING HUANG NEVER SEES ANYONE. HE DEVOTES ALL HIS TIME TO DEFENDING US.
THINK ABOUT IT... IF WE CAN HELP YOUR SOVEREIGN TO DEFEAT THE FIREBIRD...
...EVERYONE WILL KNOW THAT IT WAS THANKS TO SHINH JOH, THE GREAT EMERALD MINER!

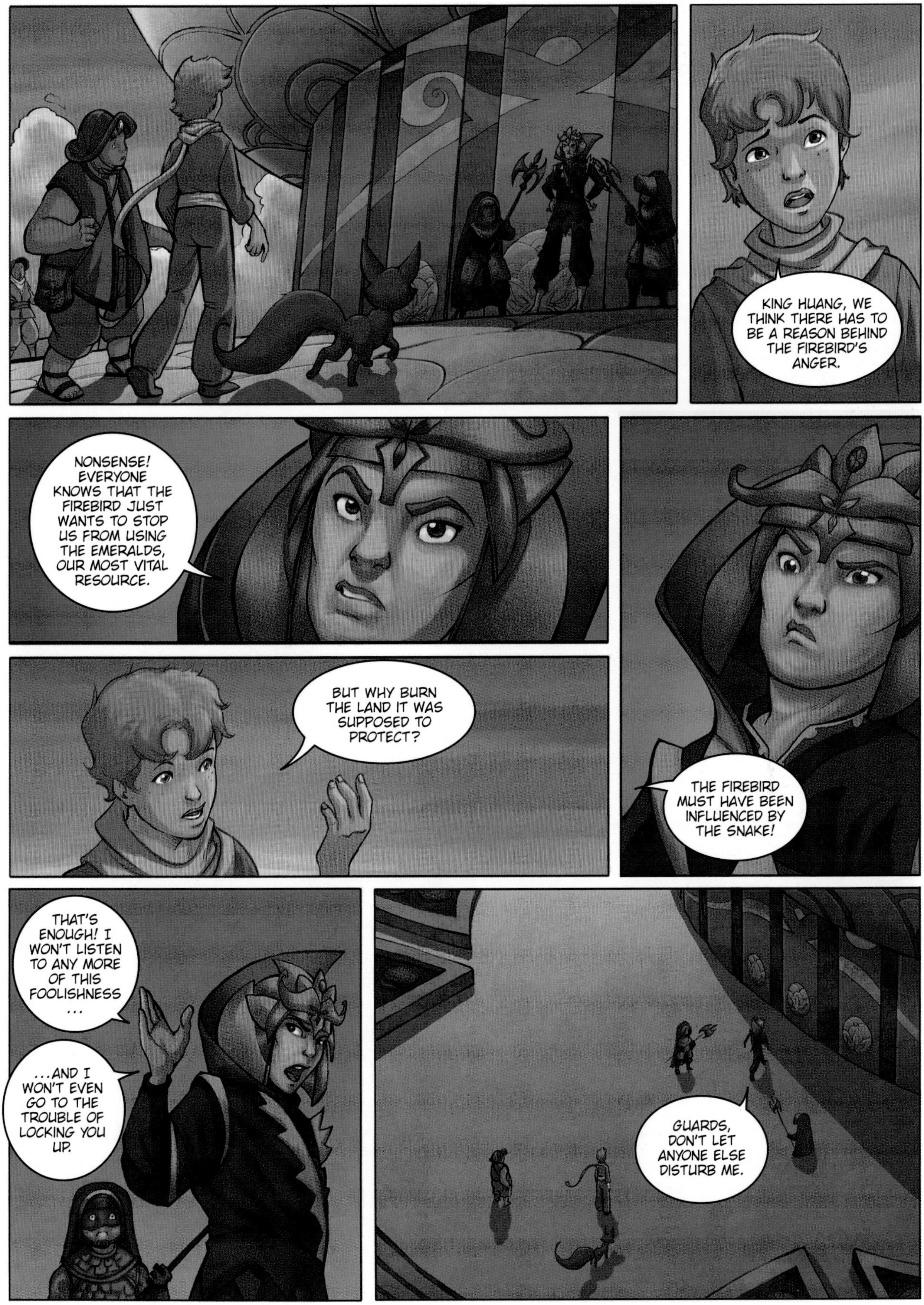
KING HUANG, WE THINK THERE HAS TO BE A REASON BEHIND THE FIREBIRD'S ANGER.
NONSENSE! EVERYONE KNOWS THAT THE FIREBIRD JUST WANTS TO STOP US FROM USING THE EMERALDS, OUR MOST VITAL RESOURCE.
BUT WHY BURN THE LAND IT WAS SUPPOSED TO PROTECT?
THE FIREBIRD MUST HAVE BEEN INFLUENCED BY THE SNAKE!
THAT'S ENOUGH! I WON'T LISTEN TO ANY MORE OF THIS FOOLISHNESS . . .
. . .AND I WON'T EVEN GO TO THE TROUBLE OF LOCKING YOU UP.
GUARDS, DON'T LET ANYONE ELSE DISTURB ME.

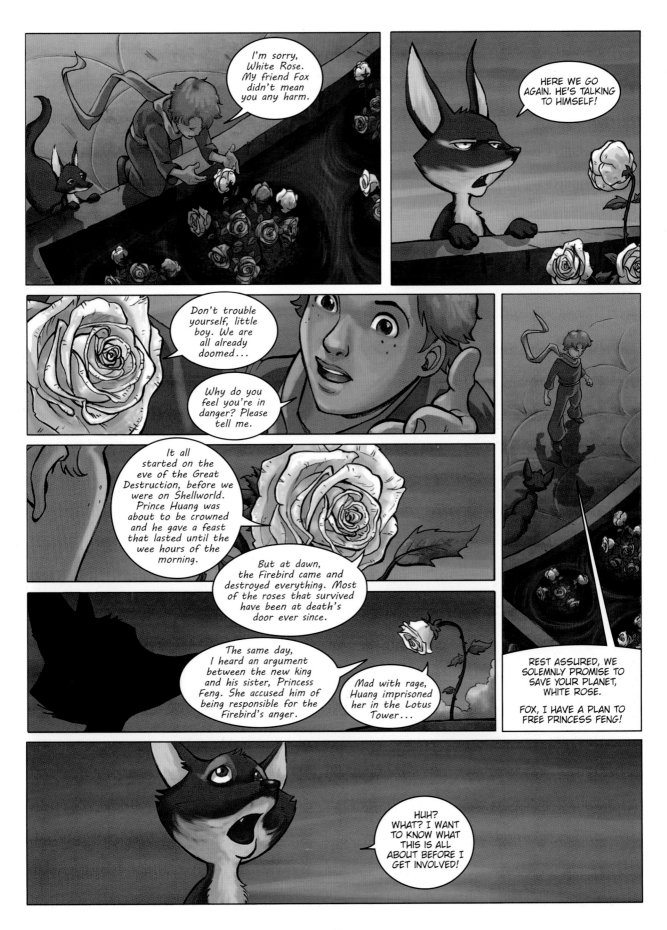

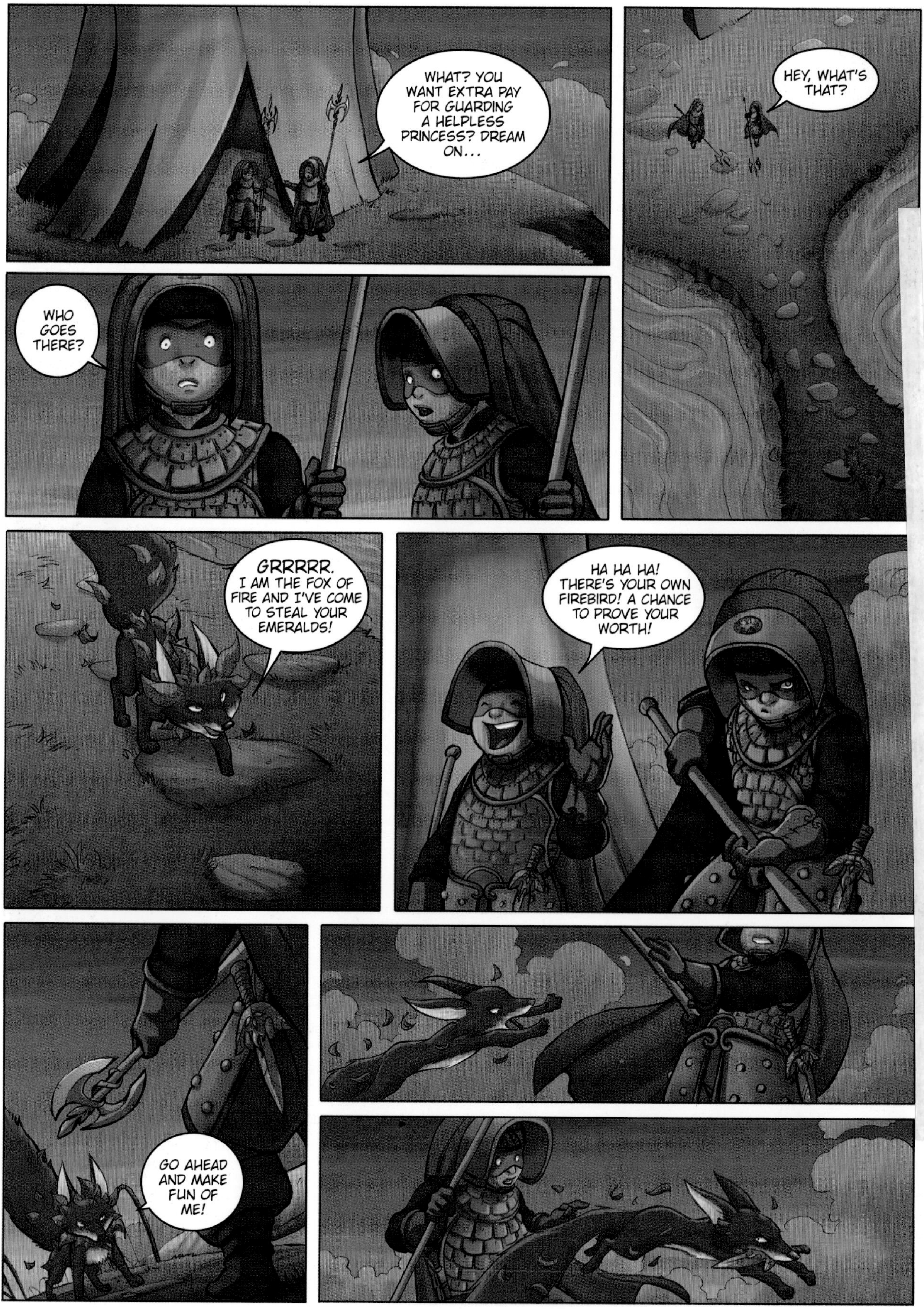

WHAT? YOU WANT EXTRA PAY FOR GUARDING A HELPLESS PRINCESS? DREAM ON...
HEY, WHAT'S THAT?
WHO GOES THERE?
GRRRRR. I AM THE FOX OF FIRE AND I'VE COME TO STEAL YOUR EMERALDS!
HA HA HA! THERE'S YOUR OWN FIREBIRD! A CHANCE TO PROVE YOUR WORTH!
GO AHEAD AND MAKE FUN OF ME!

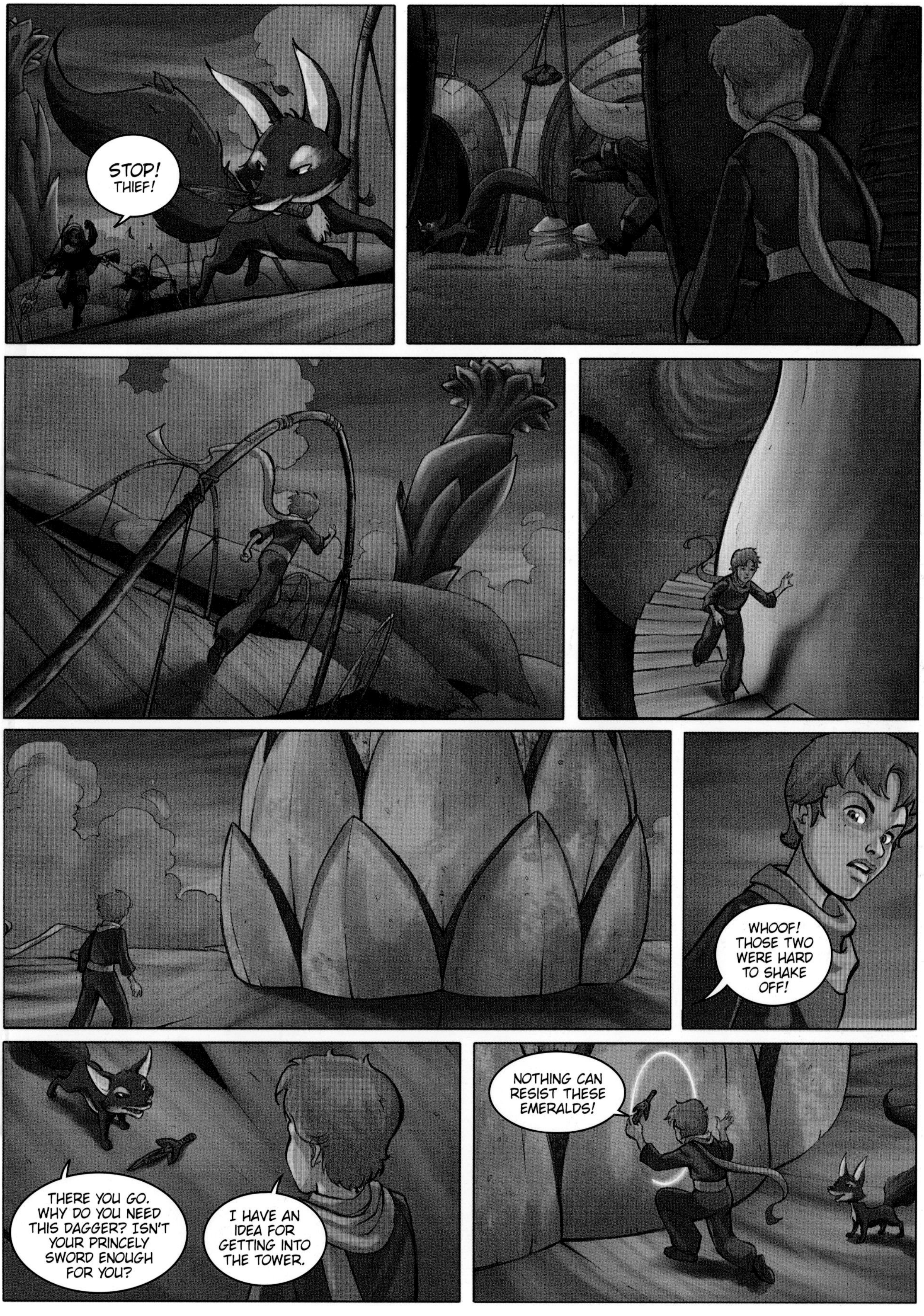
STOP! THIEF!
WHOOF! THOSE TWO WERE HARD TO SHAKE OFF!
THERE YOU GO. WHY DO YOU NEED THIS DAGGER? ISN'T YOUR PRINCELY SWORD ENOUGH FOR YOU?
I HAVE AN IDEA FOR GETTING INTO THE TOWER.
NOTHING CAN RESIST THESE EMERALDS!

FOR YEARS, TRADITION DICTATED THAT THE ROYAL FAMILY MAKE A VISIT TO THE FIREBIRD. IT WOULD FLY DOWN FROM ITS MOUNTAIN, MOUNT IZU, TO COMMUNICATE WITH US...

...BUT THIS TIME, IT WASN'T JUST A COURTESY CALL.

ON THE CONTRARY. IT'S IMPORTANT TO BE CLOSE TO ONE'S SUBJECTS.

PLEASE, PRINCESS, YOU DON'T HAVE TO DO THAT.

EVEN IF EVERYONE DOESN'T SHARE MY OPINION...

STILL TRYING TO MAKE FRIENDS, SISTER? A GOOD LEADER MUST KEEP HIS DISTANCE FROM THE PEOPLE!

YOU'LL NEVER BE A GOOD KING, THINKING LIKE THAT!

DON'T WORRY, CHILDREN. I'VE FINISHED WITH OUR OLD FRIEND.

BUT DO YOU KNOW WHERE FATHER IS? IT'S BEEN HOURS SINCE HE WENT TO SEE THE FIREBIRD.

FATHER! YOU TOOK SO LONG... WHAT DID YOU HAVE THAT WAS SO IMPORTANT TO DISCUSS WITH OUR FRIEND?

COME. I HAVE VERY SAD NEWS TO GIVE YOU.

I TOLD IT THAT, SINCE I AM UNABLE TO MAKE A CHOICE, IT MUST DECIDE IN MY PLACE, WHEN IT JUDGES THAT ONE OF YOU IS READY.

THE FIREBIRD HAS TOLD ME THAT MY LIFE HAS ALMOST REACHED ITS END AND HAS ASKED ME TO CHOOSE AN HEIR.

BREAKING THIS SOLEMN PACT IN ANY WAY WILL BRING DOWN ITS ANGER!

23

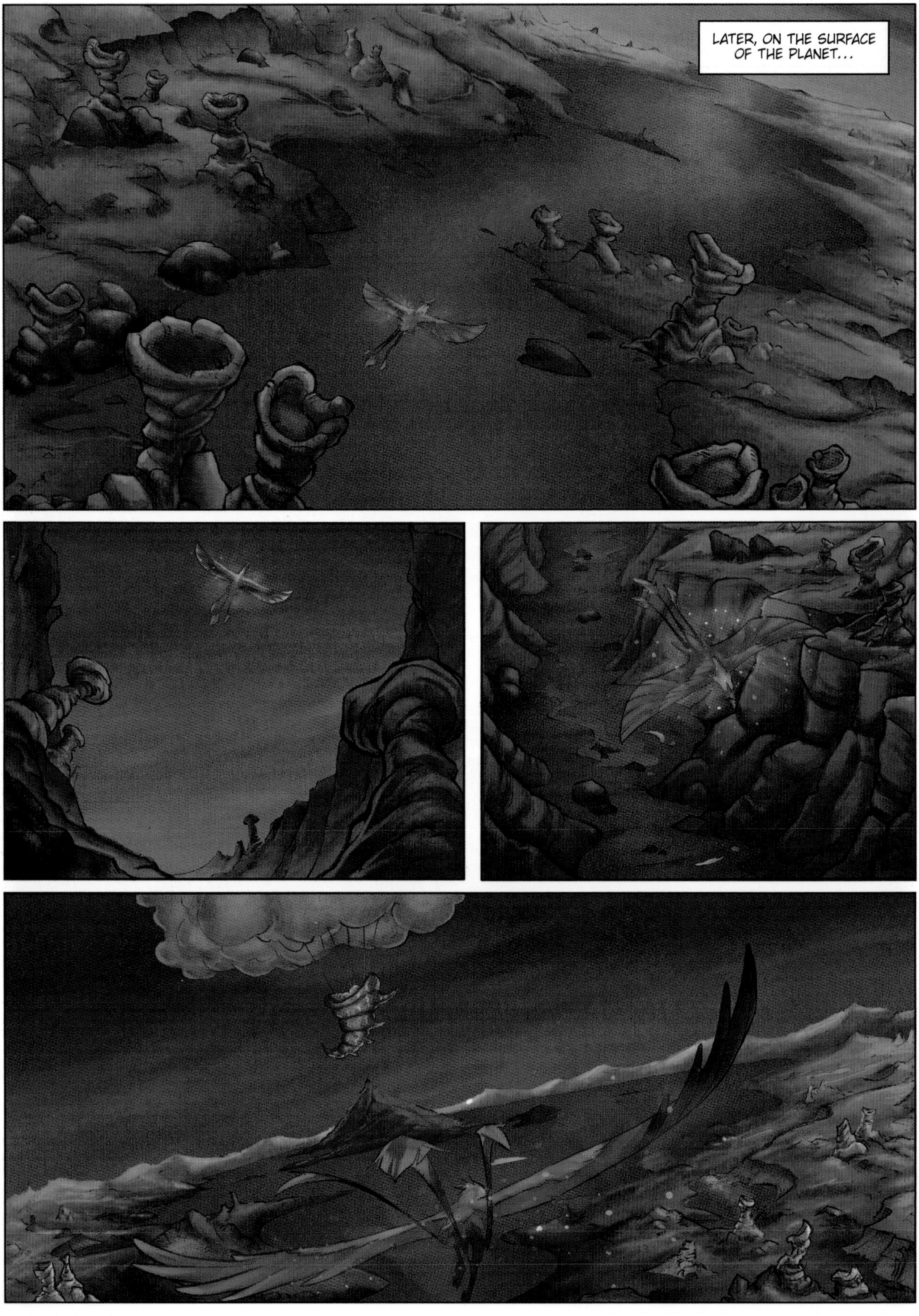
LATER, ON THE SURFACE OF THE PLANET...

THE FIREBIRD IS BACK! EVERYONE GET UNDER COVER!

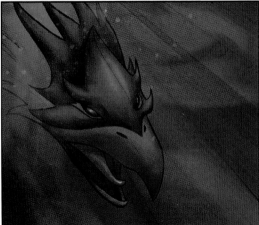

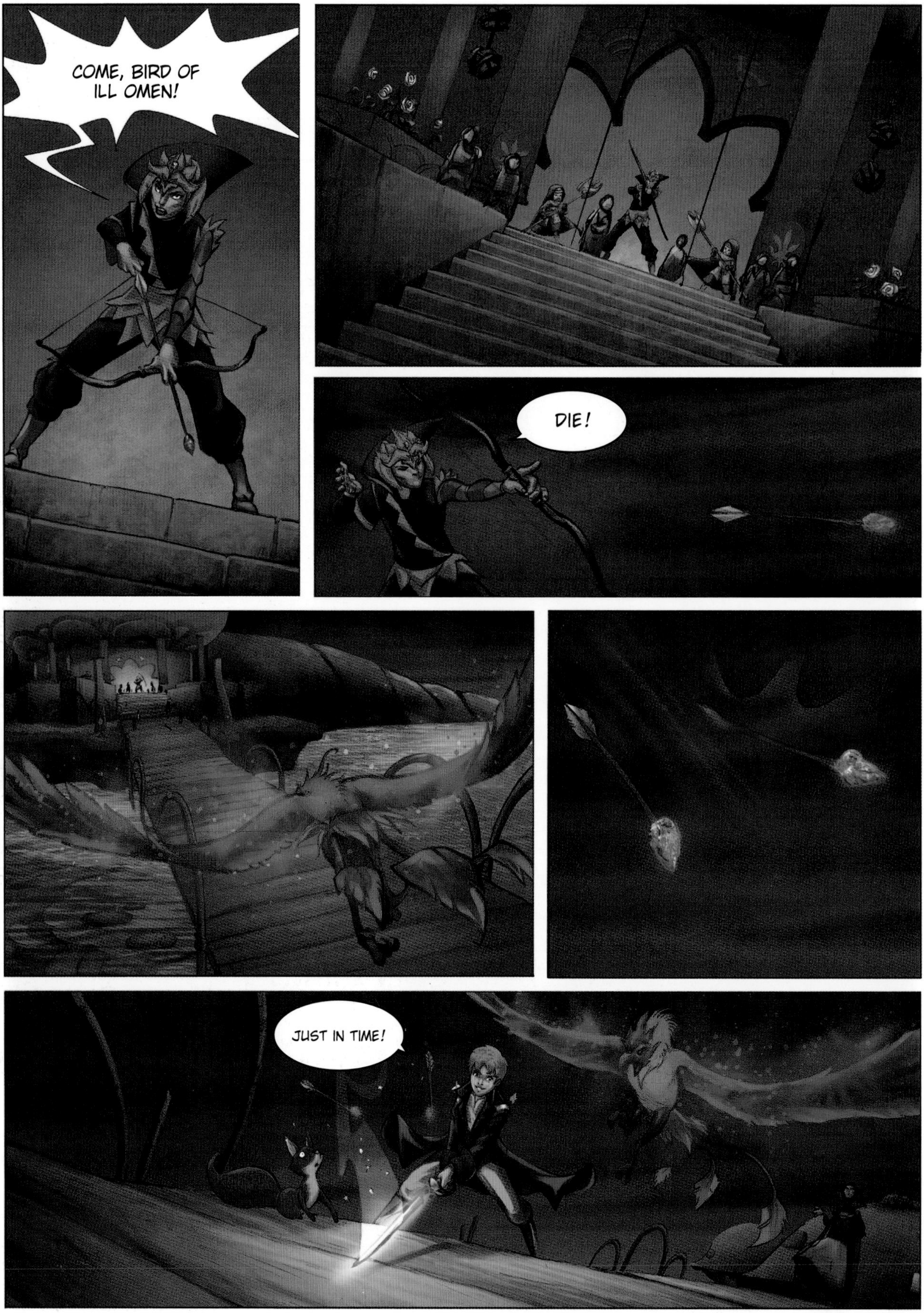
COME, BIRD OF ILL OMEN!
DIE!
JUST IN TIME!

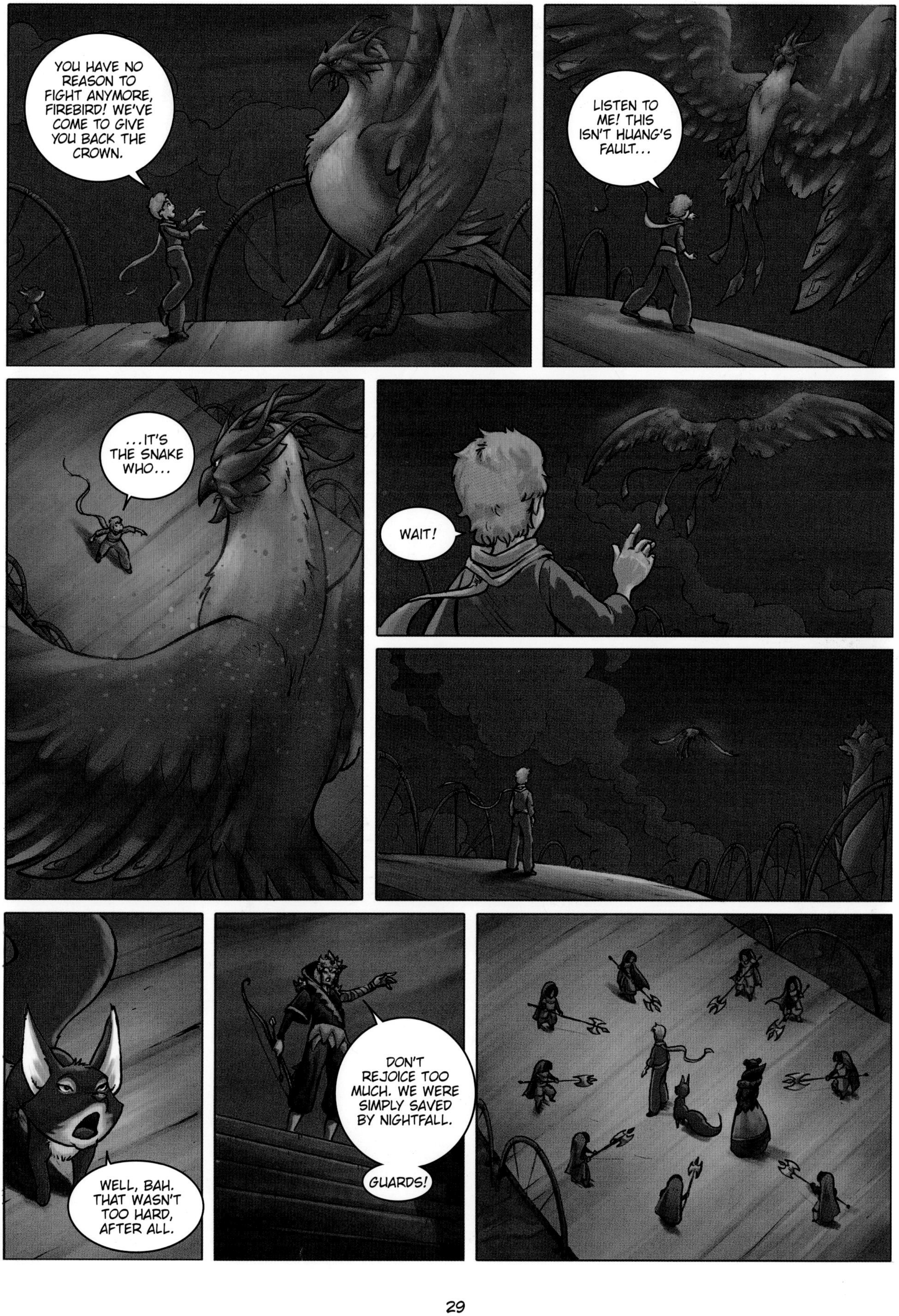
YOU HAVE NO REASON TO FIGHT ANYMORE, FIREBIRD! WE'VE COME TO GIVE YOU BACK THE CROWN.
LISTEN TO ME! THIS ISN'T HUANG'S FAULT...
...IT'S THE SNAKE WHO...
WAIT!
WELL, BAH. THAT WASN'T TOO HARD, AFTER ALL.
DON'T REJOICE TOO MUCH. WE WERE SIMPLY SAVED BY NIGHTFALL.
GUARDS!

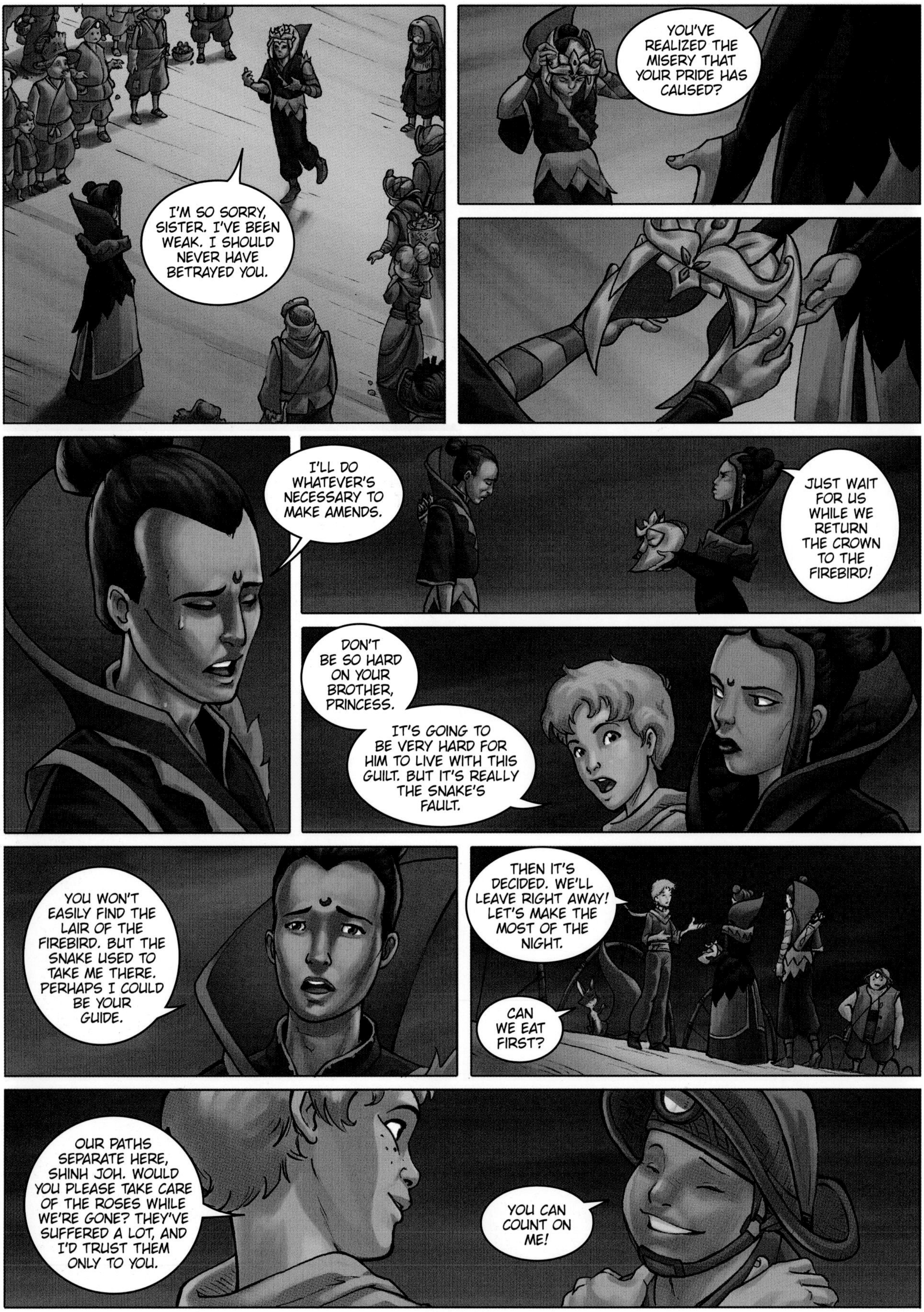
I'M SO SORRY, SISTER. I'VE BEEN WEAK. I SHOULD NEVER HAVE BETRAYED YOU.
YOU'VE REALIZED THE MISERY THAT YOUR PRIDE HAS CAUSED?
I'LL DO WHATEVER'S NECESSARY TO MAKE AMENDS.
JUST WAIT FOR US WHILE WE RETURN THE CROWN TO THE FIREBIRD!
DON'T BE SO HARD ON YOUR BROTHER, PRINCESS.
IT'S GOING TO BE VERY HARD FOR HIM TO LIVE WITH THIS GUILT. BUT IT'S REALLY THE SNAKE'S FAULT.
YOU WON'T EASILY FIND THE LAIR OF THE FIREBIRD. BUT THE SNAKE USED TO TAKE ME THERE. PERHAPS I COULD BE YOUR GUIDE.
THEN IT'S DECIDED. WE'LL LEAVE RIGHT AWAY! LET'S MAKE THE MOST OF THE NIGHT.
CAN WE EAT FIRST?
OUR PATHS SEPARATE HERE, SHINH JOH. WOULD YOU PLEASE TAKE CARE OF THE ROSES WHILE WE'RE GONE? THEY'VE SUFFERED A LOT, AND I'D TRUST THEM ONLY TO YOU.
YOU CAN COUNT ON ME!

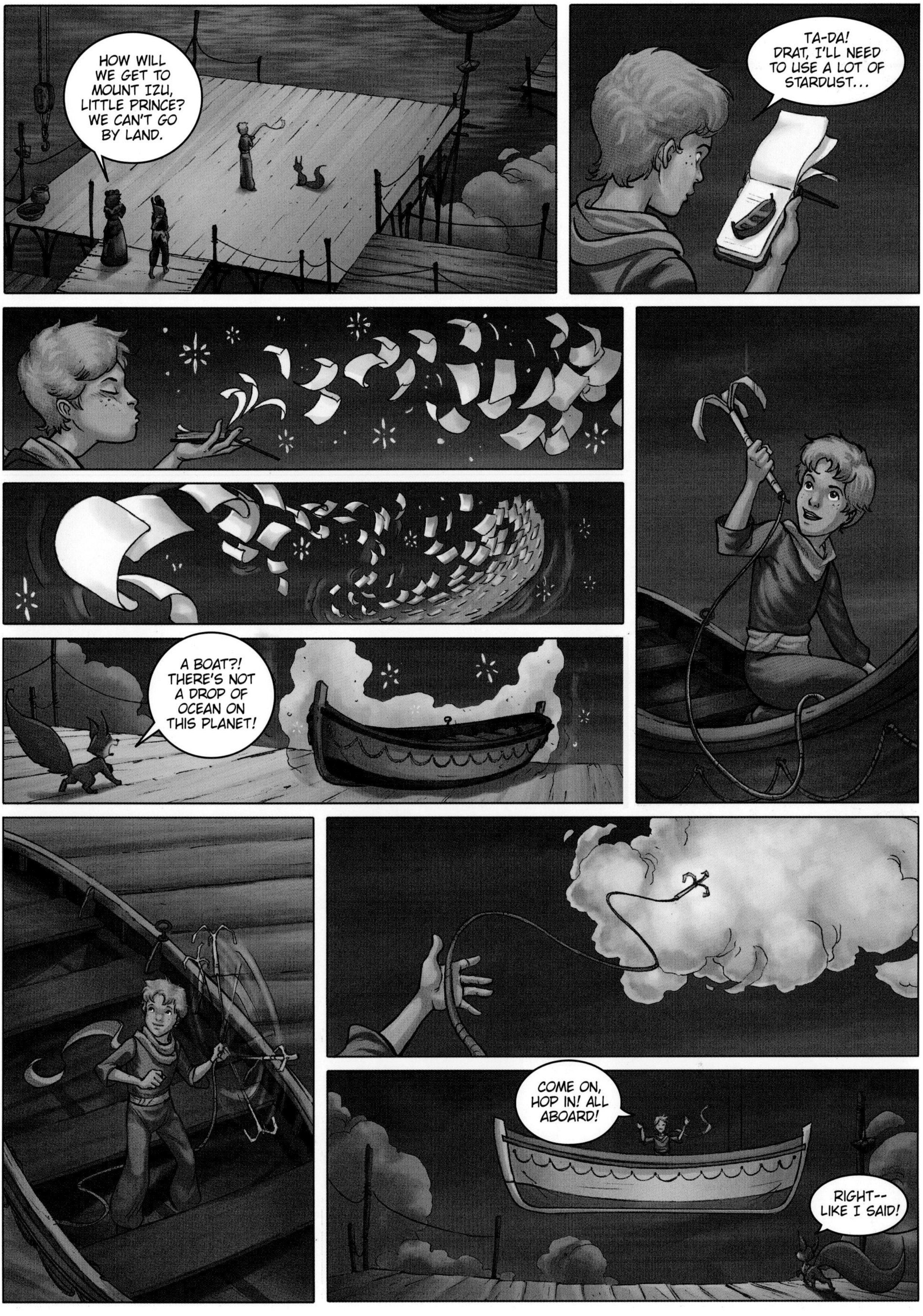
HOW WILL WE GET TO MOUNT IZU, LITTLE PRINCE? WE CAN'T GO BY LAND.
TA-DA! DRAT, I'LL NEED TO USE A LOT OF STARDUST...
A BOAT?! THERE'S NOT A DROP OF OCEAN ON THIS PLANET!
COME ON, HOP IN! ALL ABOARD!
RIGHT-- LIKE I SAID!

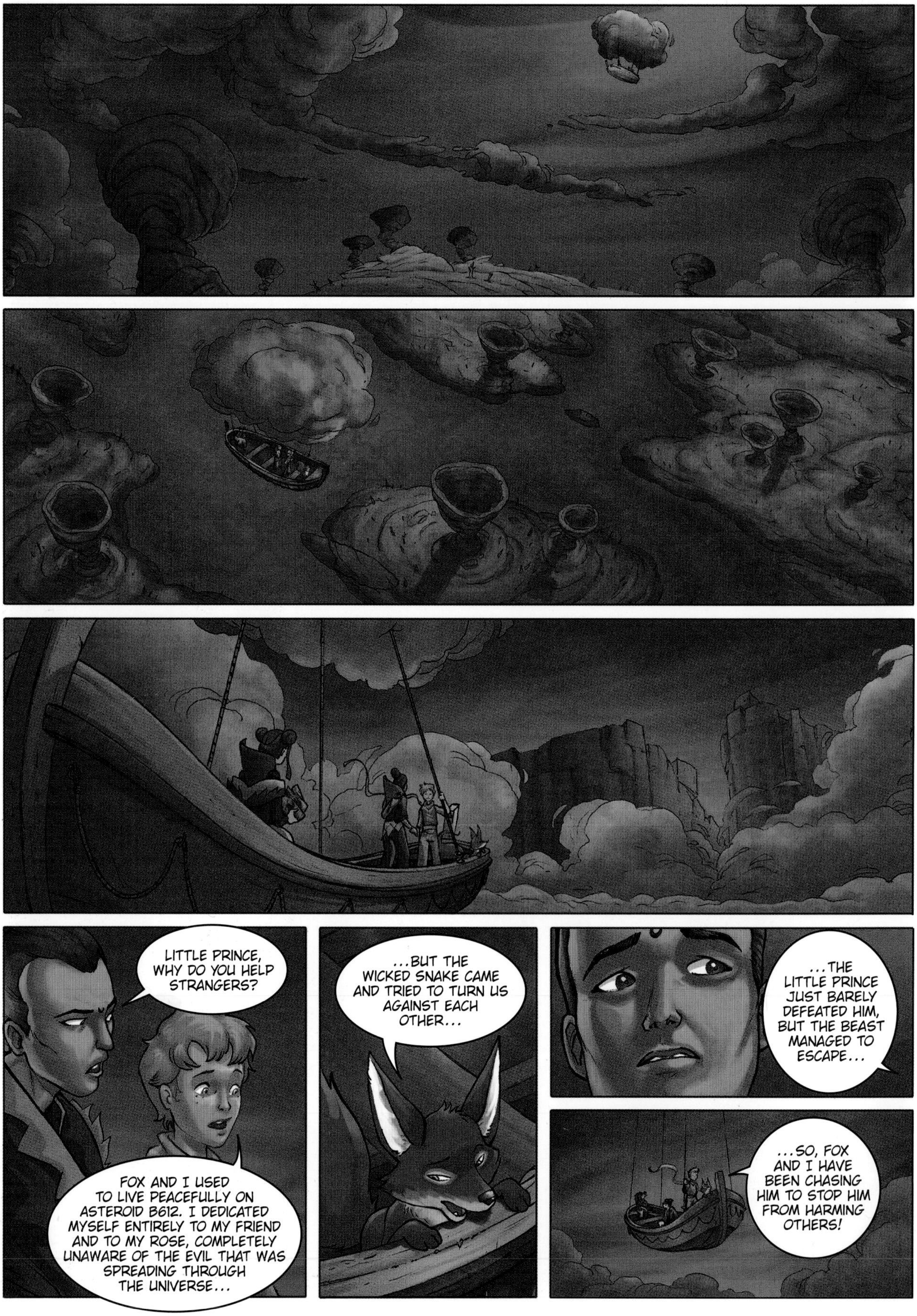
LITTLE PRINCE, WHY DO YOU HELP STRANGERS?
FOX AND I USED TO LIVE PEACEFULLY ON ASTEROID B612. I DEDICATED MYSELF ENTIRELY TO MY FRIEND AND TO MY ROSE, COMPLETELY UNAWARE OF THE EVIL THAT WAS SPREADING THROUGH THE UNIVERSE...
...BUT THE WICKED SNAKE CAME AND TRIED TO TURN US AGAINST EACH OTHER...
...THE LITTLE PRINCE JUST BARELY DEFEATED HIM, BUT THE BEAST MANAGED TO ESCAPE...
...SO, FOX AND I HAVE BEEN CHASING HIM TO STOP HIM FROM HARMING OTHERS!

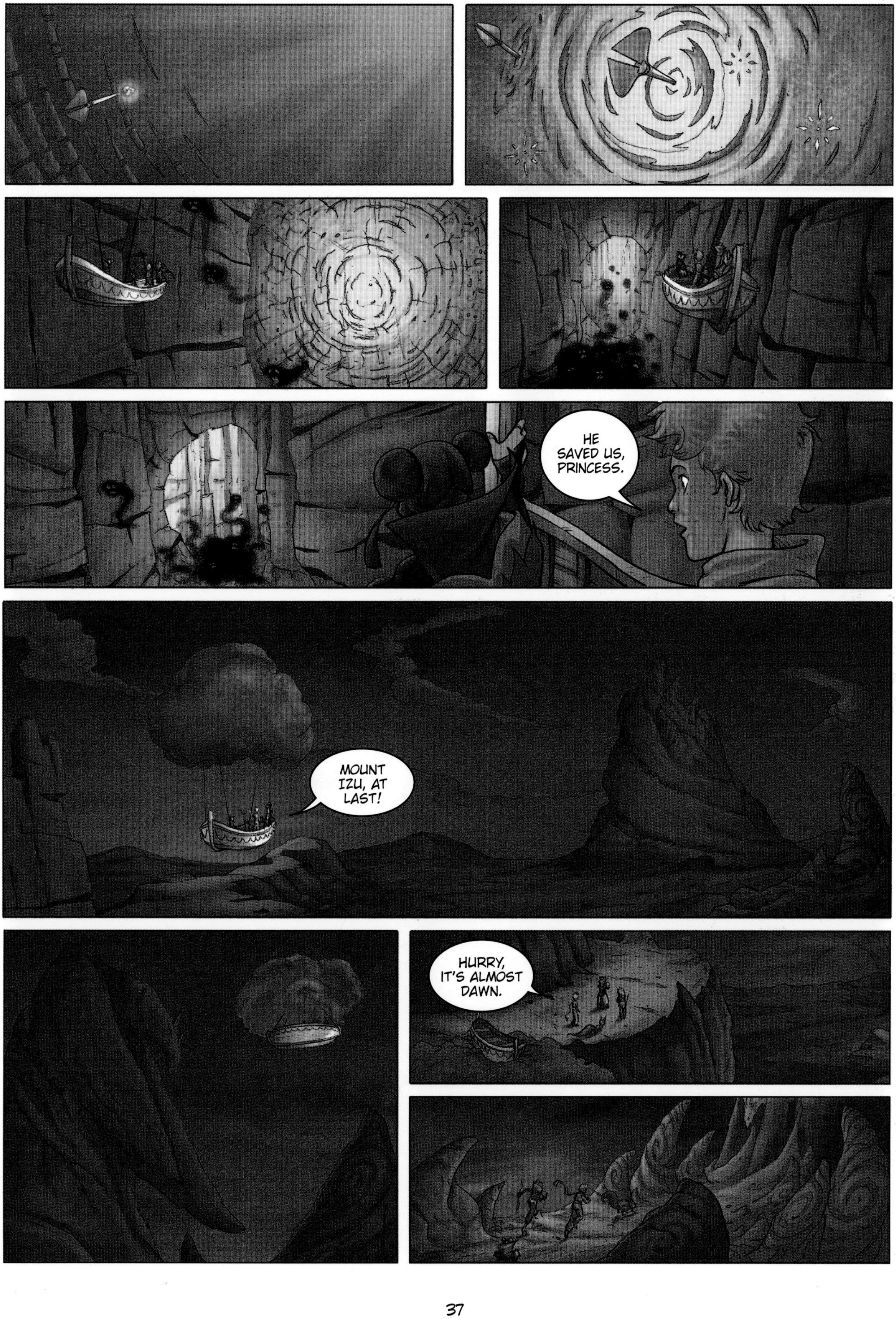
HE SAVED US, PRINCESS.
MOUNT IZU, AT LAST!
HURRY, IT'S ALMOST DAWN.

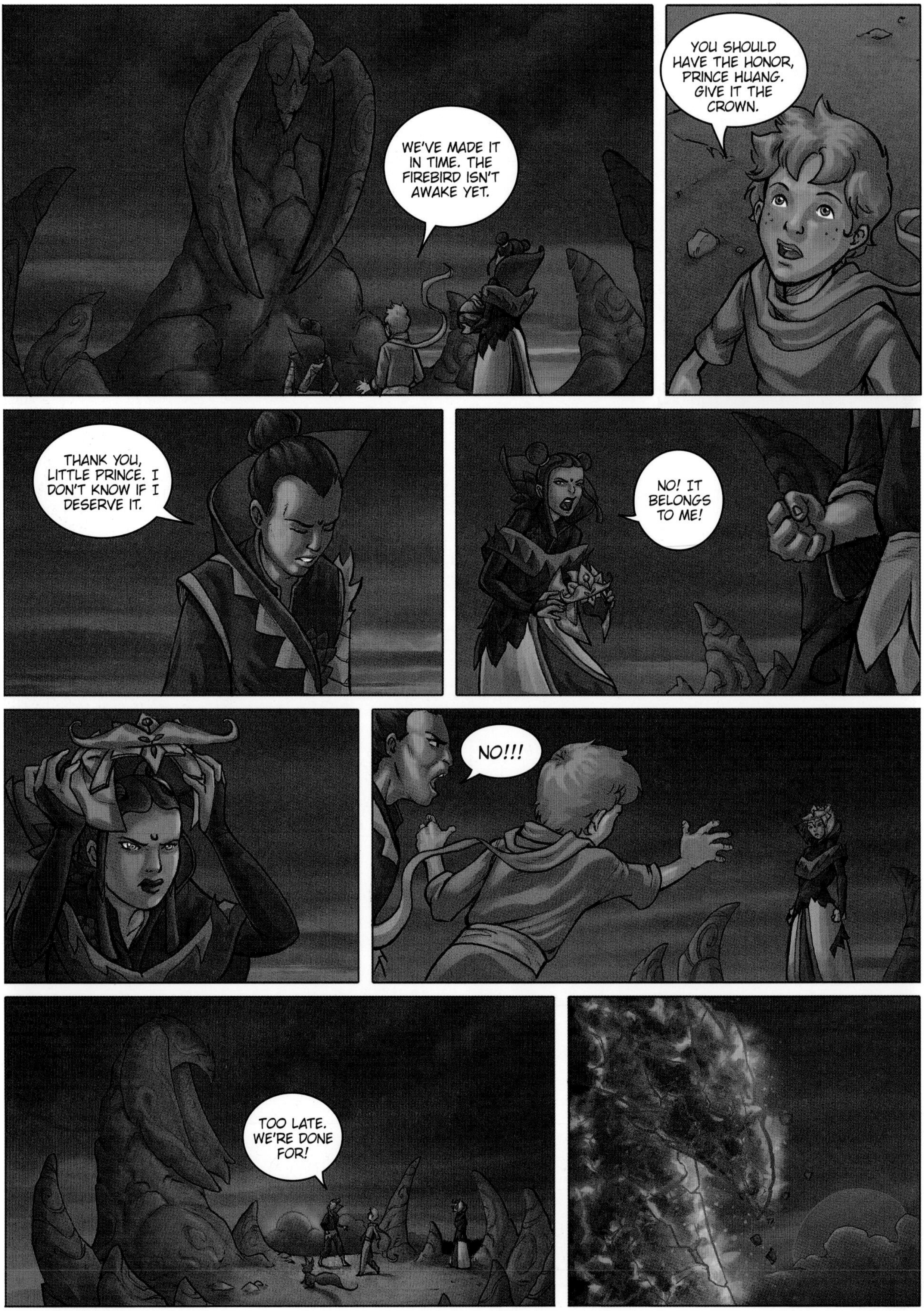
WE'VE MADE IT IN TIME. THE FIREBIRD ISN'T AWAKE YET.
YOU SHOULD HAVE THE HONOR, PRINCE HUANG. GIVE IT THE CROWN.
THANK YOU, LITTLE PRINCE. I DON'T KNOW IF I DESERVE IT.
NO! IT BELONGS TO ME!
NO!!!
TOO LATE. WE'RE DONE FOR!

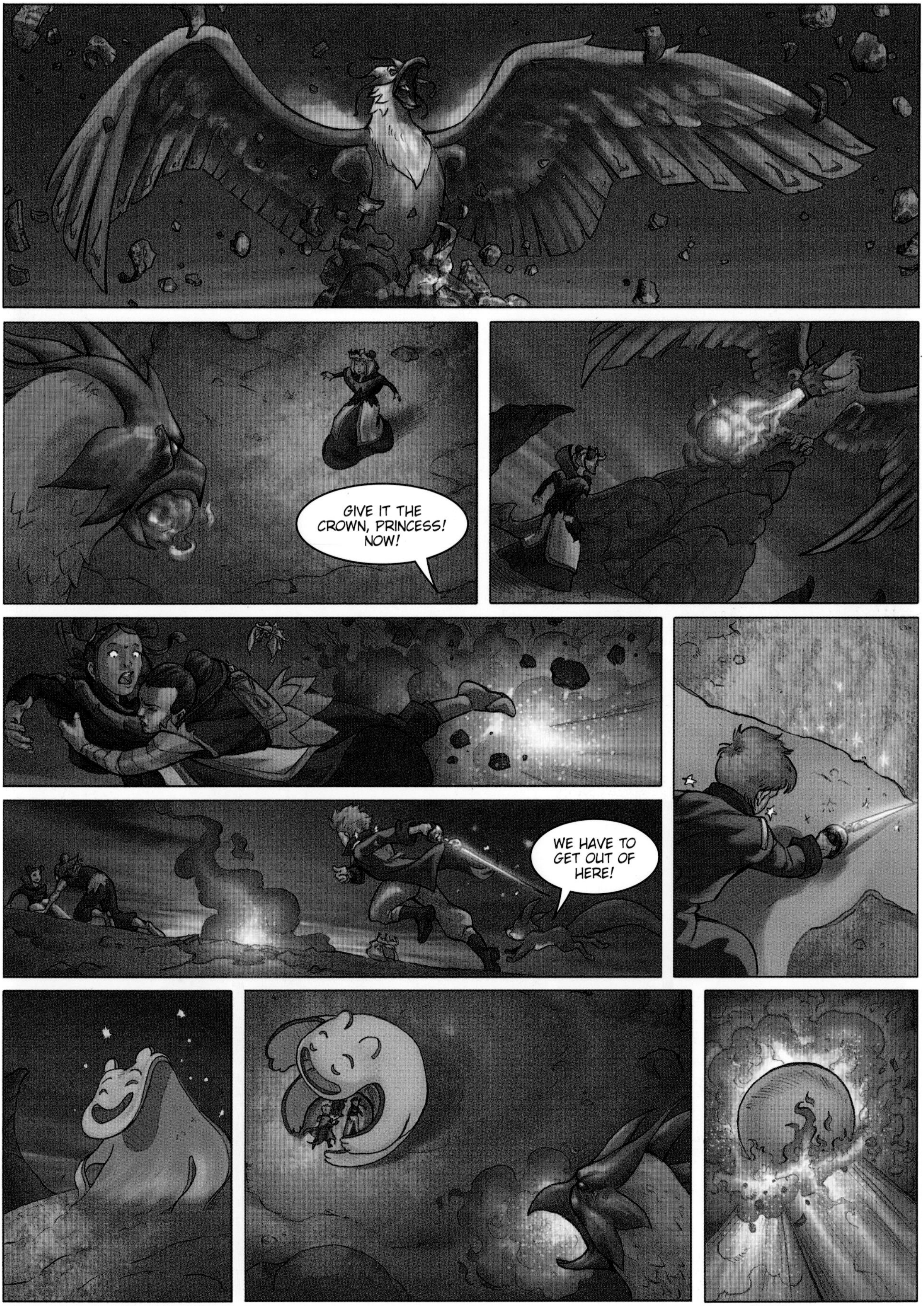
GIVE IT THE CROWN, PRINCESS! NOW!
WE HAVE TO GET OUT OF HERE!

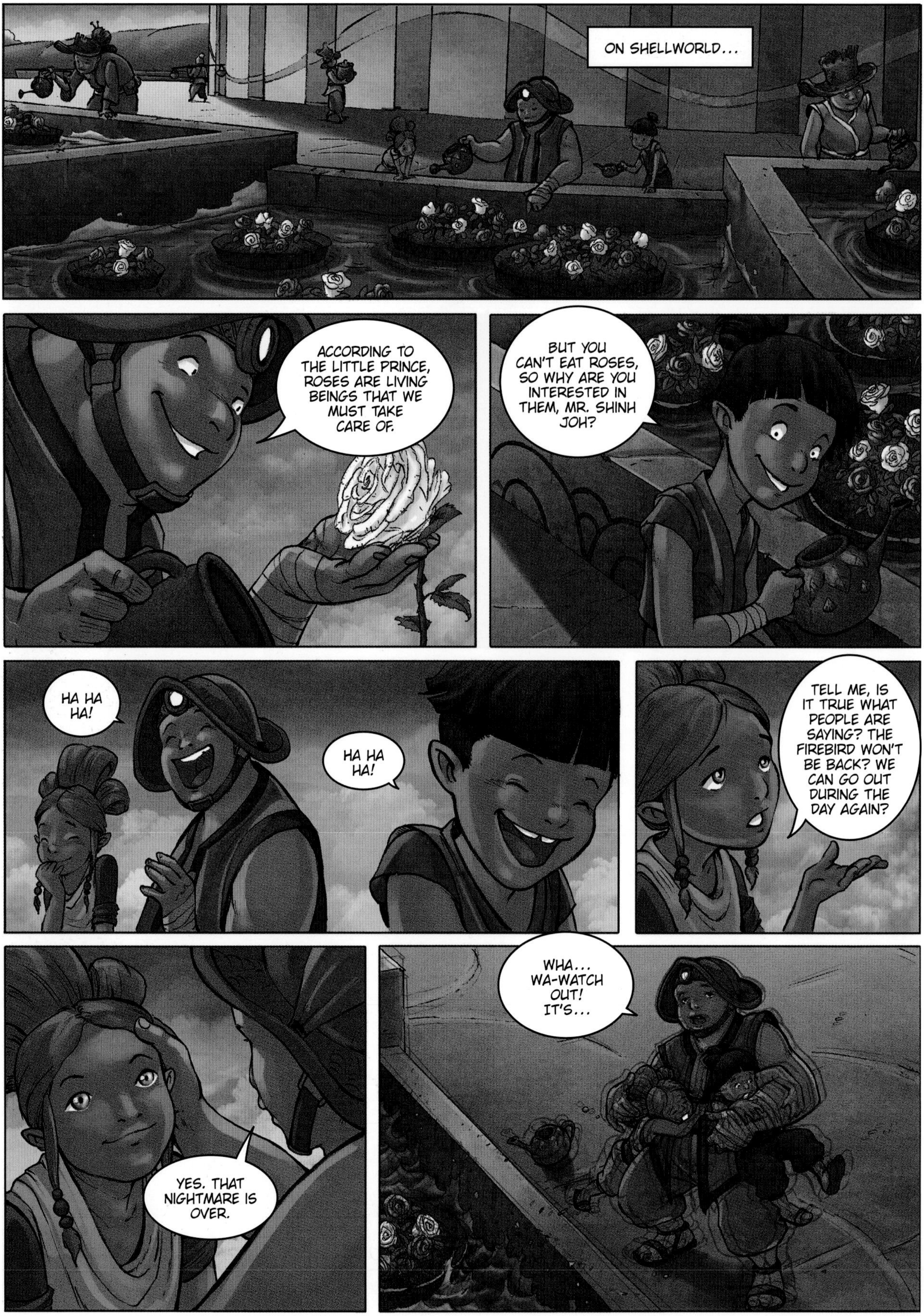
ON SHELLWORLD...
ACCORDING TO THE LITTLE PRINCE, ROSES ARE LIVING BEINGS THAT WE MUST TAKE CARE OF.
BUT YOU CAN'T EAT ROSES, SO WHY ARE YOU INTERESTED IN THEM, MR. SHINH JOH?
HA HA HA!
HA HA HA!
TELL ME, IS IT TRUE WHAT PEOPLE ARE SAYING? THE FIREBIRD WON'T BE BACK? WE CAN GO OUT DURING THE DAY AGAIN?
YES. THAT NIGHTMARE IS OVER.
WHA... WA-WATCH OUT! IT'S...

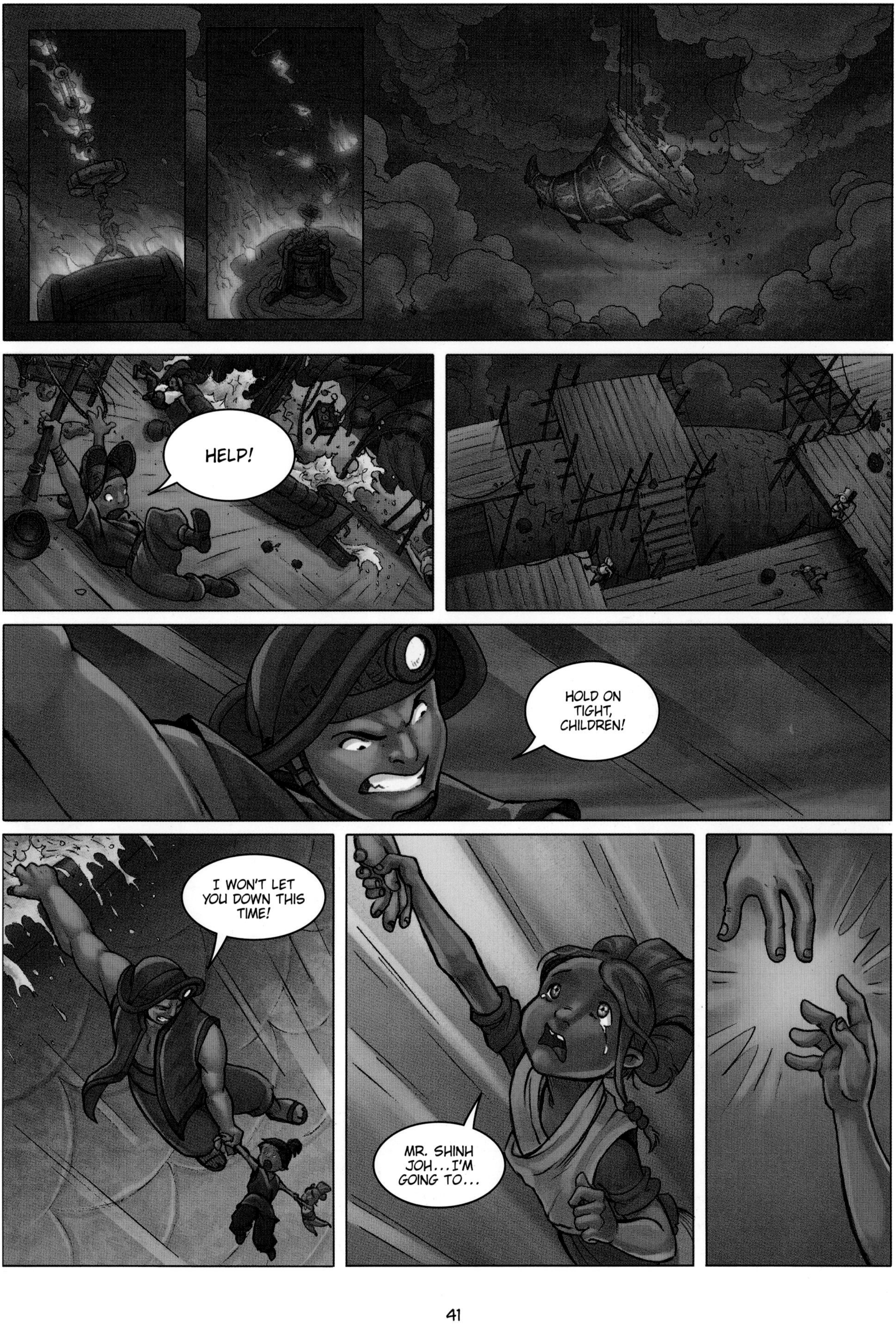
HELP!
HOLD ON TIGHT, CHILDREN!
I WON'T LET YOU DOWN THIS TIME!
MR. SHINH JOH...I'M GOING TO...

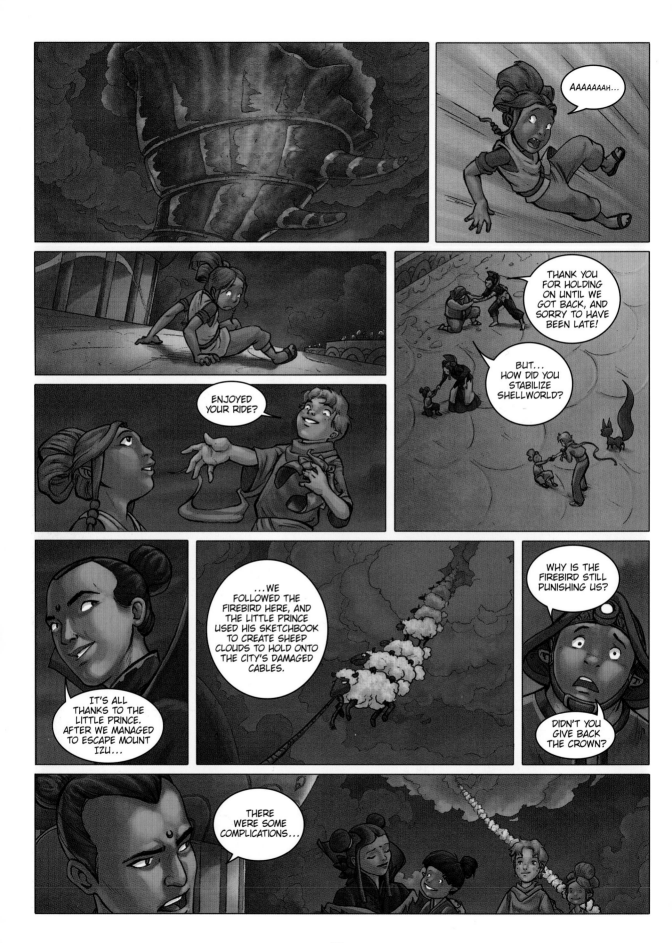

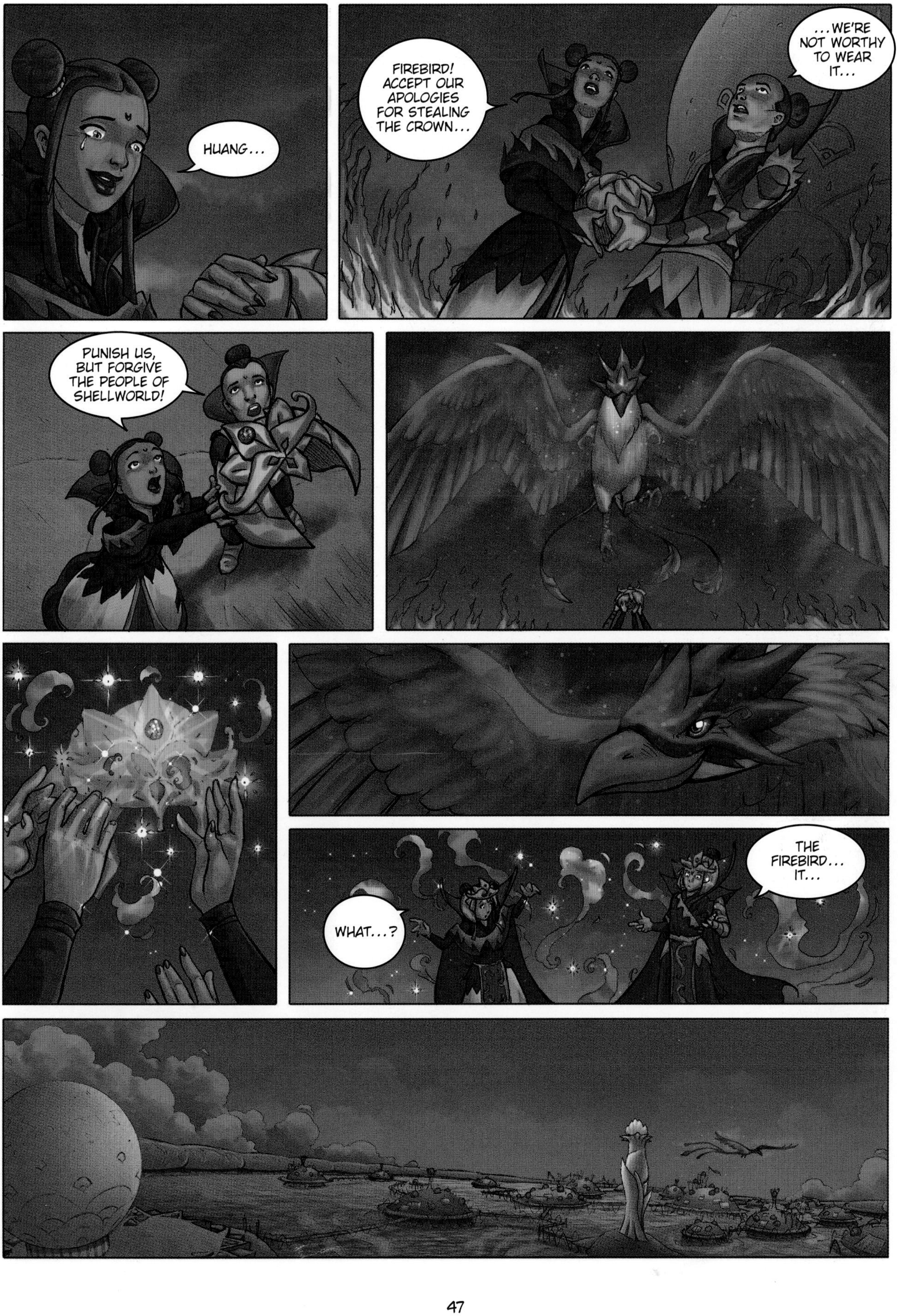
HUANG...
FIREBIRD! ACCEPT OUR APOLOGIES FOR STEALING THE CROWN...
...WE'RE NOT WORTHY TO WEAR IT...
PUNISH US, BUT FORGIVE THE PEOPLE OF SHELLWORLD!
THE FIREBIRD... IT...
WHAT...?

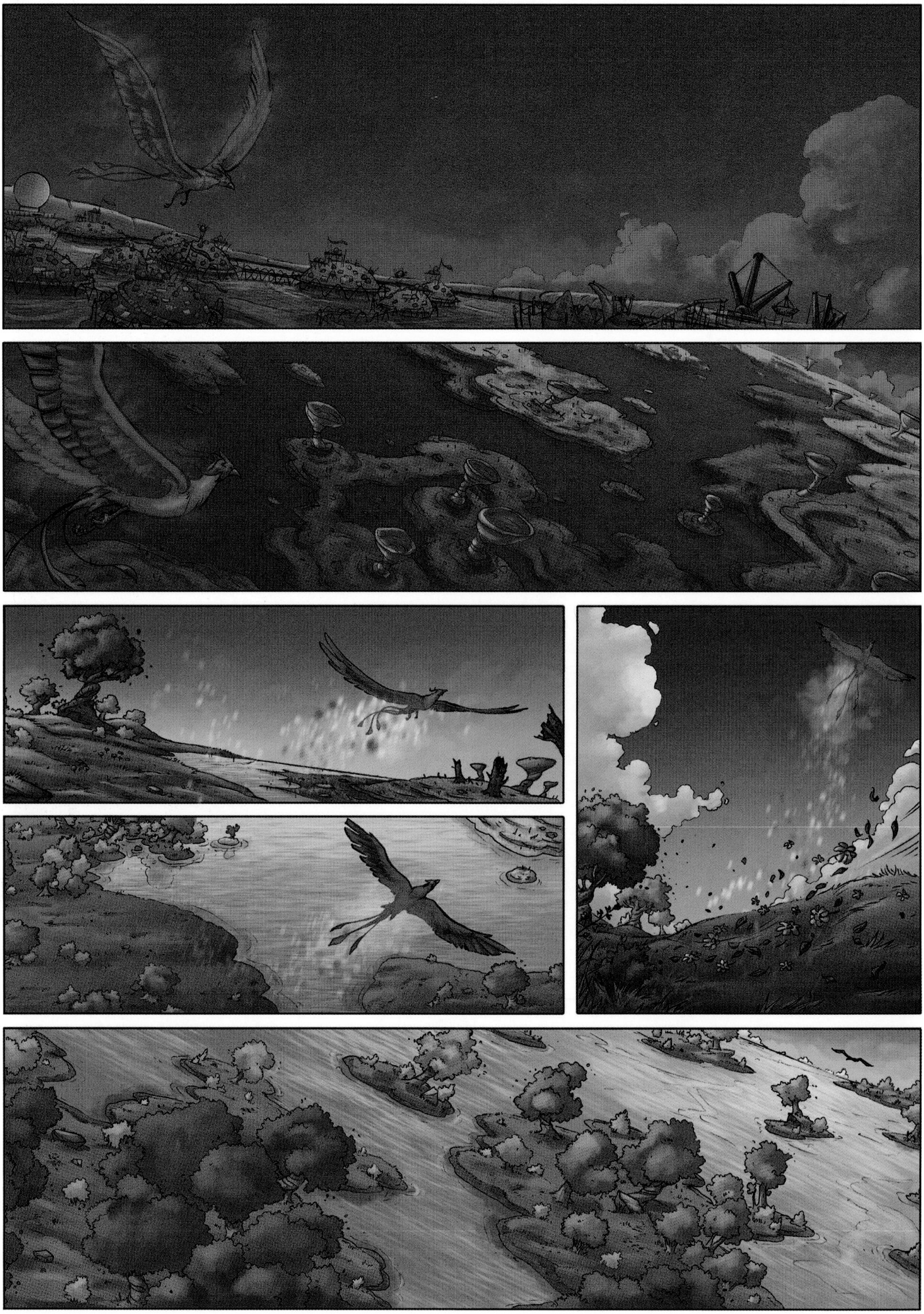

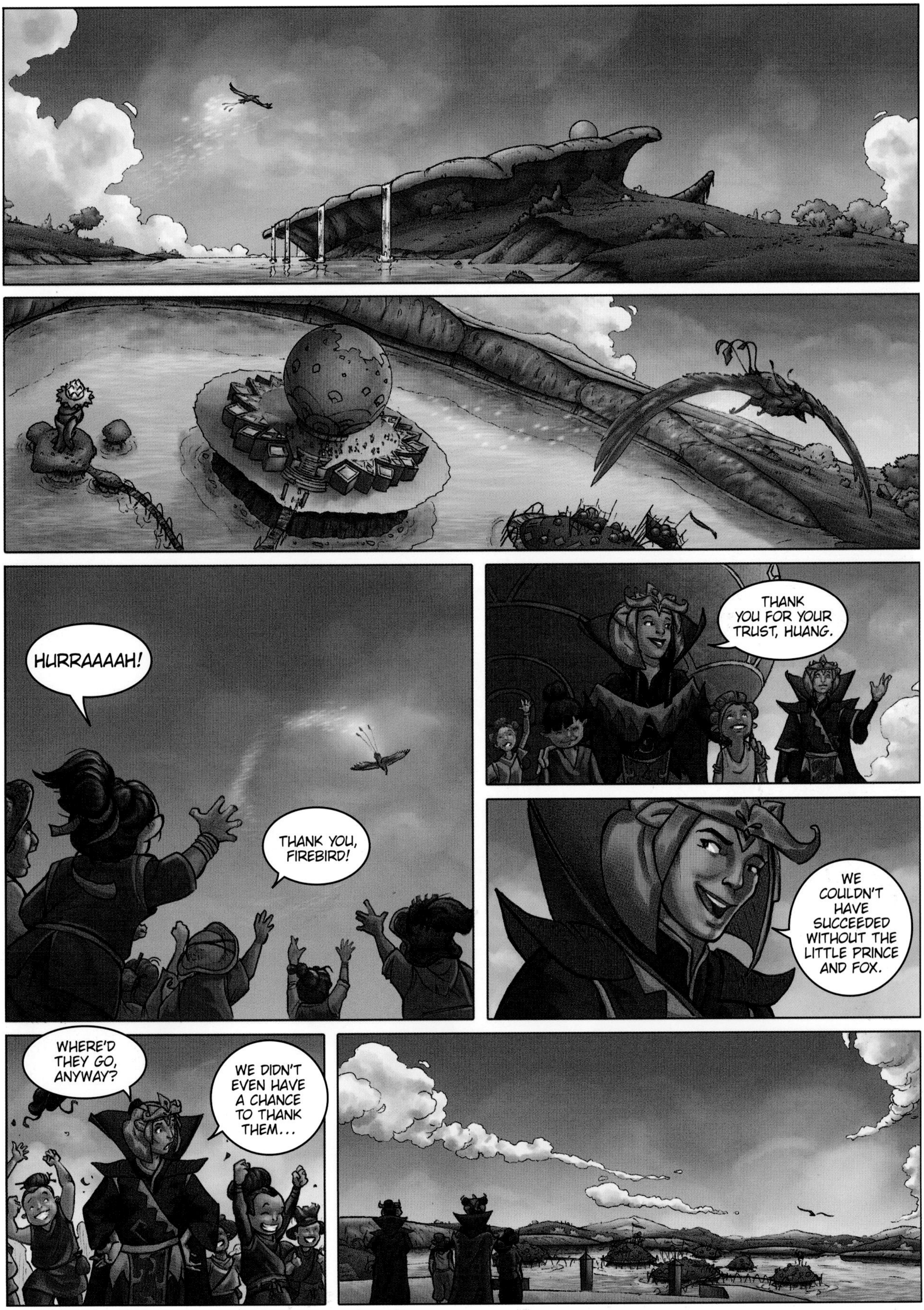
HURRAAAAH!
THANK YOU, FIREBIRD!
THANK YOU FOR YOUR TRUST, HUANG.
WE COULDN'T HAVE SUCCEEDED WITHOUT THE LITTLE PRINCE AND FOX.
WHERE'D THEY GO, ANYWAY?
WE DIDN'T EVEN HAVE A CHANCE TO THANK THEM...

THE END

The Little Prince

AS IMAGINED BY

TEBO

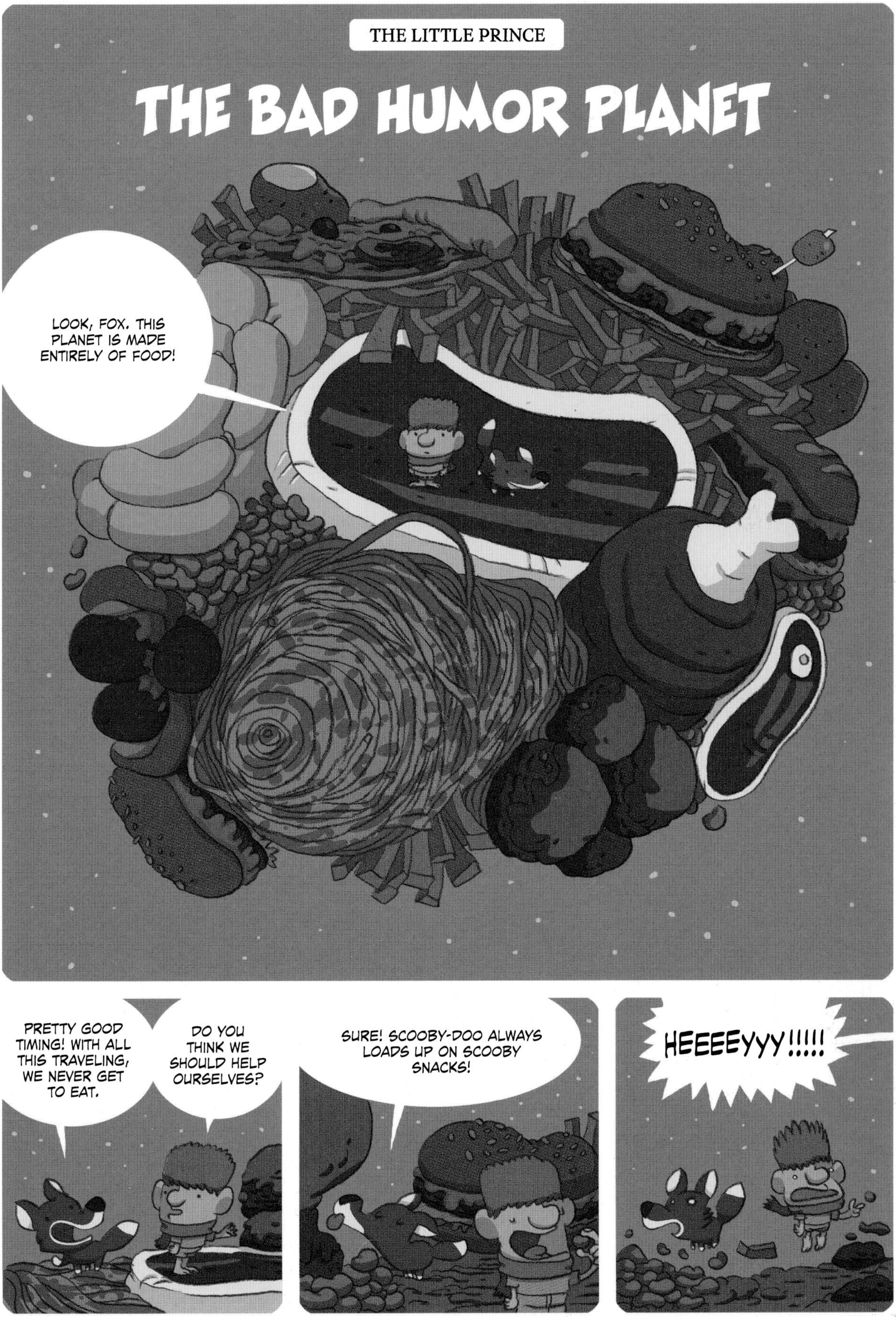
THE LITTLE PRINCE
THE BAD HUMOR PLANET
LOOK, FOX. THIS PLANET IS MADE ENTIRELY OF FOOD!
PRETTY GOOD TIMING! WITH ALL THIS TRAVELING, WE NEVER GET TO EAT.
DO YOU THINK WE SHOULD HELP OURSELVES?
SURE! SCOOBY-DOO ALWAYS LOADS UP ON SCOOBY SNACKS!
HEEEEyyy!!!!!

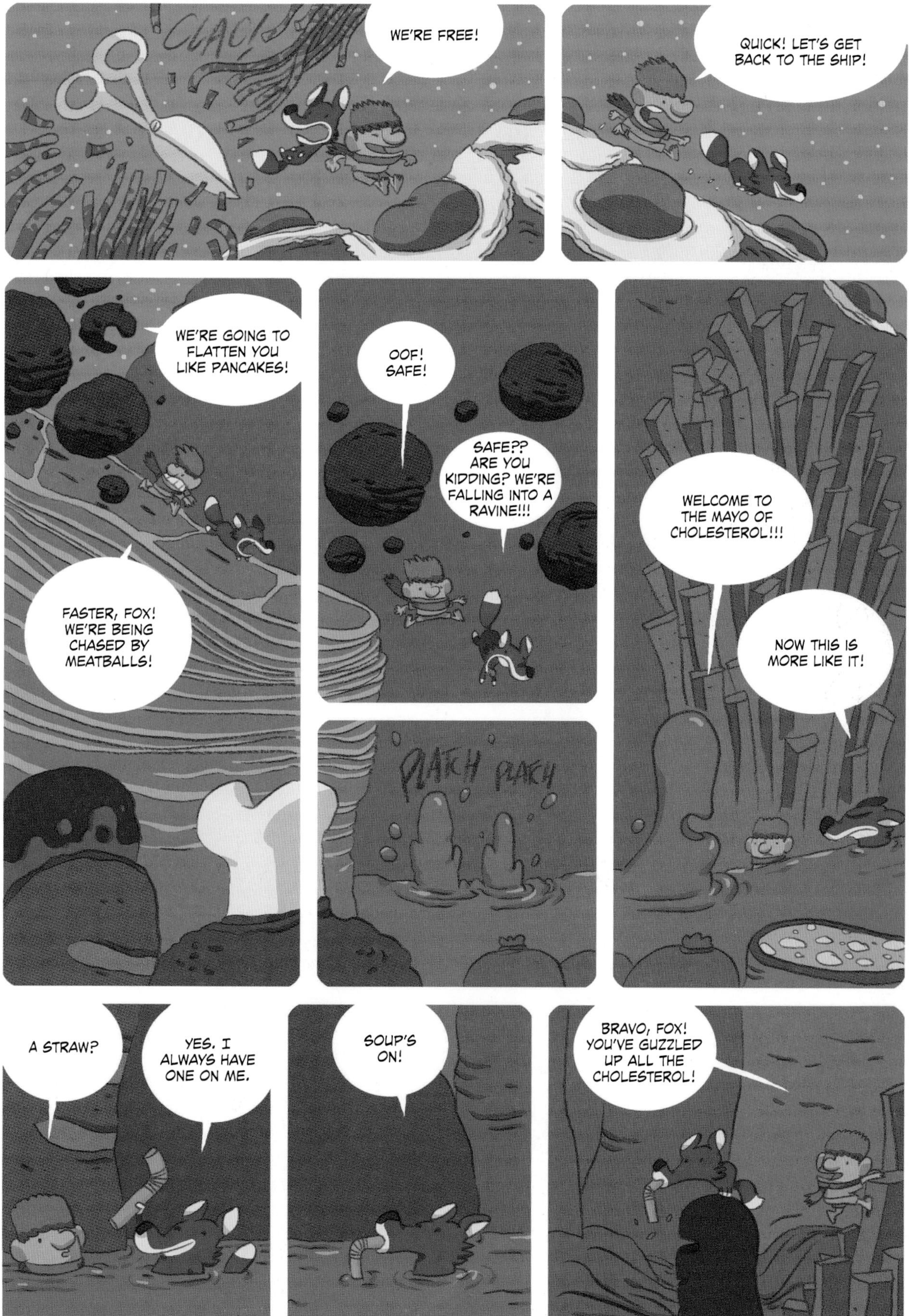
CLAC!
WE'RE FREE!
QUICK! LET'S GET BACK TO THE SHIP!
WE'RE GOING TO FLATTEN YOU LIKE PANCAKES!
FASTER, FOX! WE'RE BEING CHASED BY MEATBALLS!
OOF! SAFE!
SAFE?? ARE YOU KIDDING? WE'RE FALLING INTO A RAVINE!!!
PLATCH PLATCH
WELCOME TO THE MAYO OF CHOLESTEROL!!!
NOW THIS IS MORE LIKE IT!
A STRAW?
YES. I ALWAYS HAVE ONE ON ME.
SOUP'S ON!
BRAVO, FOX! YOU'VE GUZZLED UP ALL THE CHOLESTEROL!

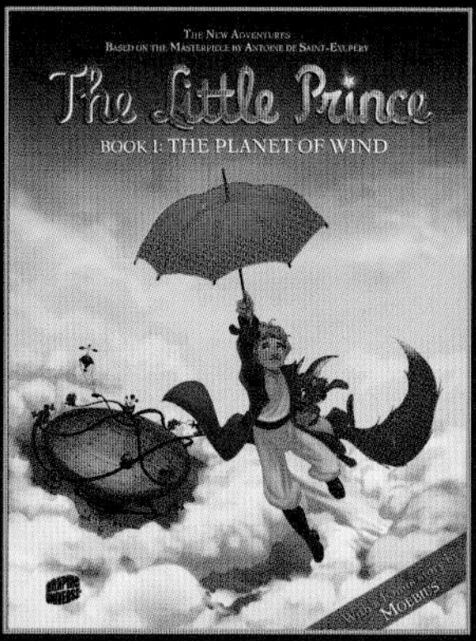
The Little Prince
BOOK 1: THE PLANET OF WIND

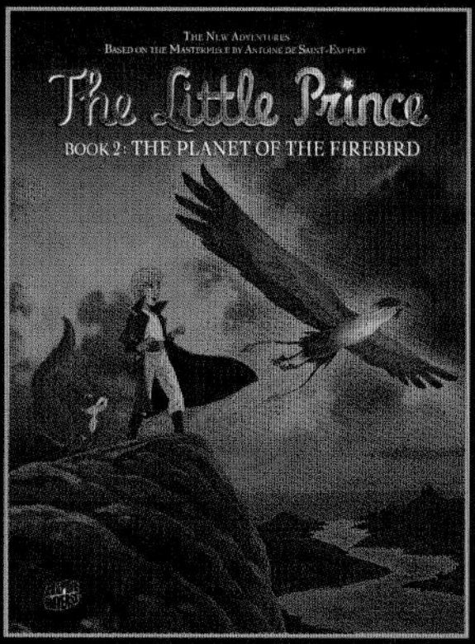
The Little Prince
BOOK 2: THE PLANET OF THE FIREBIRD

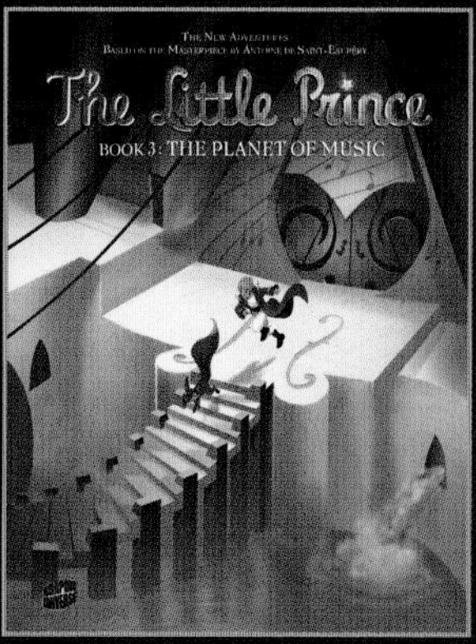
The Little Prince
BOOK 3: THE PLANET OF MUSIC

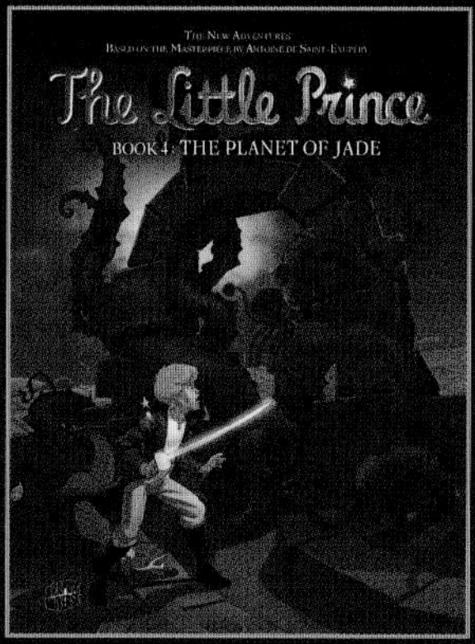
The Little Prince
BOOK 4: THE PLANET OF JADE

BOOK 1: THE PLANET OF WIND

BOOK 2: THE PLANET OF THE FIREBIRD

BOOK 3: THE PLANET OF MUSIC

BOOK 4: THE PLANET OF JADE

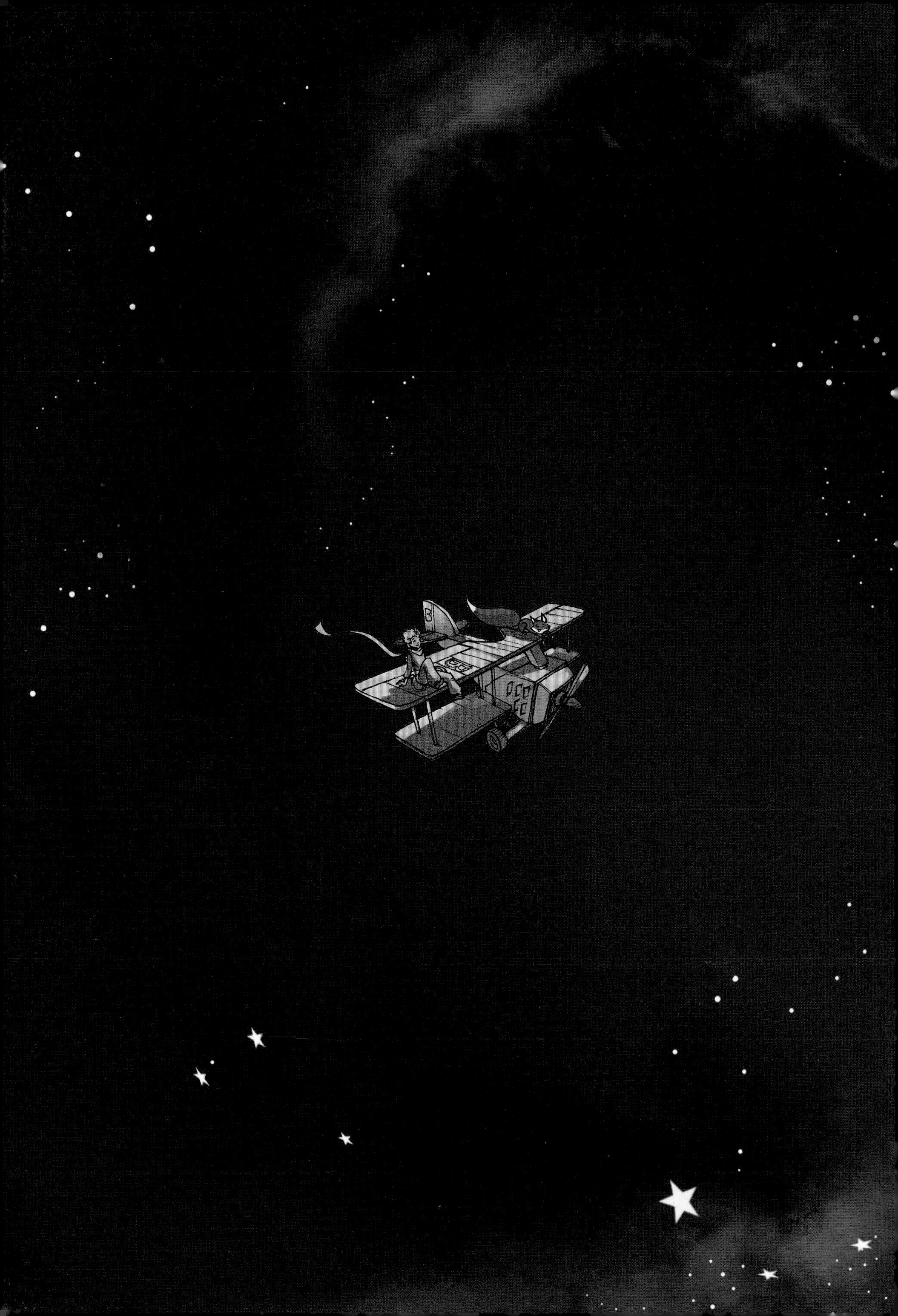

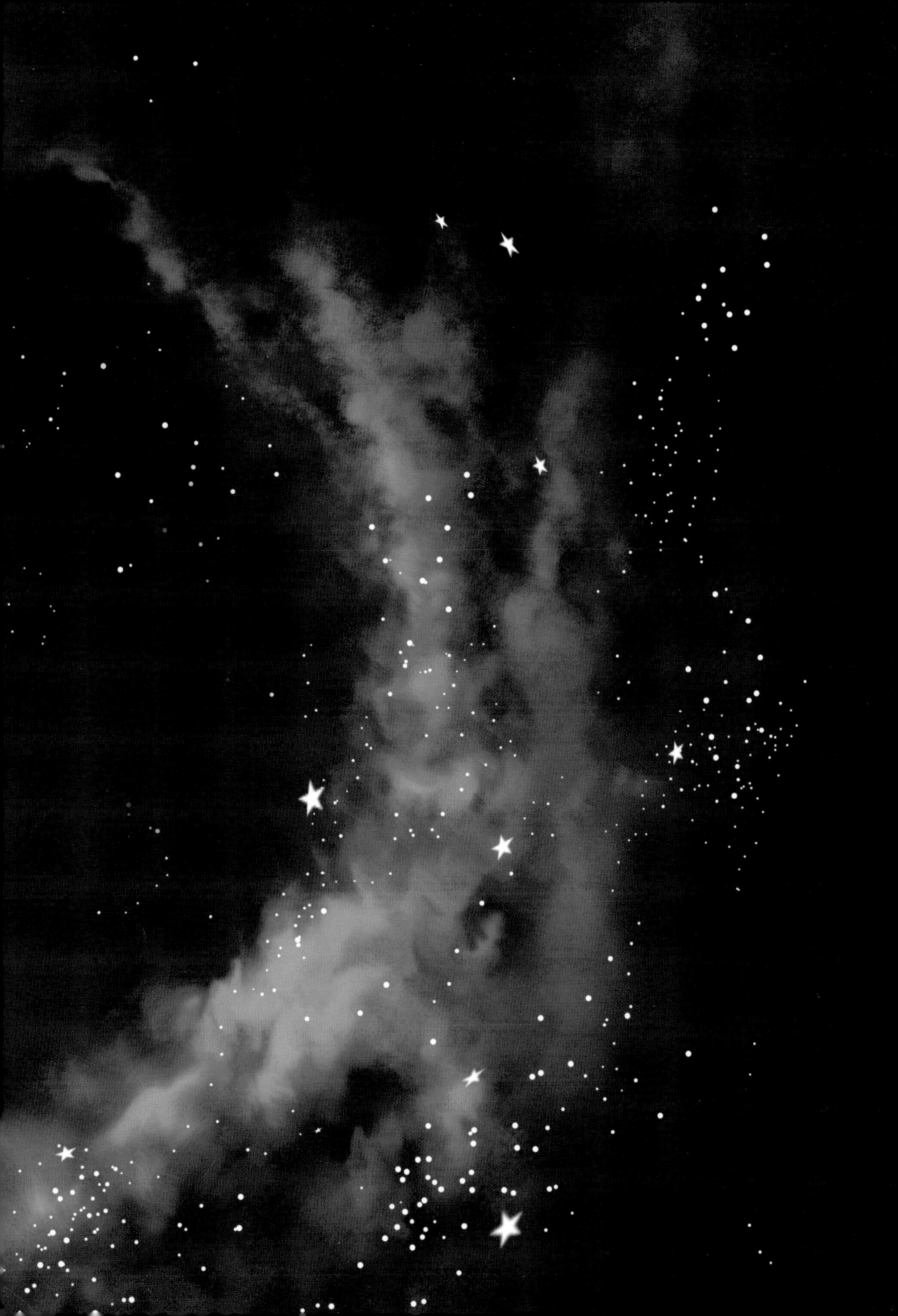